BETWEEN & BETWIXT

THE CORRIDOR OF DOORS TRILOGY - BOOK 1

B & T PECILE

 **FriesenPress**

Suite 300 - 990 Fort St

Victoria, BC, Canada, V8V 3K2

www.friesenpress.com

Copyright © 2015 by Bruno Pecile & Tina Pecile

First Edition — 2015

This book is a work of fiction...

ISBN

978-1-4602-6607-6 (Hardcover)

978-1-4602-6608-3 (Paperback)

978-1-4602-6609-0 (eBook)

1. Fiction, Fantasy

Distributed to the trade by The Ingram Book Company

Table of Contents

Prologue

i

CHAPTER 1

Strange and Unfamiliar Places

1

CHAPTER 2

Poor Old Meg

5

CHAPTER 3

Dodger and Goula

11

CHAPTER 4

Pond

17

CHAPTER 5

Father Tobias

23

CHAPTER 6

Norbert and McBride

31

CHAPTER 7

Road Trip

37

CHAPTER 8

Something Evil Rises

45

CHAPTER 9

Lady's Knight

55

CHAPTER 10

The Weight and Width of a Ticket

65

CHAPTER 11

Into the Dark Dark Forest

71

CHAPTER 12

A Home in the Wilderness

79

CHAPTER 13

A World Without Light

83

CHAPTER 14

Timothea

93

CHAPTER 15

The Pendant

97

CHAPTER 16

The Fourth Apprentice

103

CHAPTER 17

Down Stream

111

CHAPTER 18

Grandfather's Song

119

CHAPTER 19

White World Malls

123

CHAPTER 20

Bridges, Boats and Trains

129

CHAPTER 21

When Clouds Descend

135

CHAPTER 22

The Westmoreland Bridge

143

CHAPTER 23

The Familiar

149

CHAPTER 24

The Sylph

157

CHAPTER 25

The Planes of Abraham

163

CHAPTER 26

Safe Houses

171

CHAPTER 27

Stalk and Strike

179

CHAPTER 28

Between Heaven and Hell

185

CHAPTER 29

Grand Central Station

193

CHAPTER 30

Sanctuary

203

Epilogue

207

Sometimes in those in-between places
Where the lights flicker on and off
In Worlds Betwixt and Worlds Between
Surprising things can happen

Sometimes in those brief stuttering moments
When time is suspended and still
In Worlds Between and Worlds Betwixt
Magical things can happen

BETWEEN
BETWIXT

&

Prologue

It was at a midpoint between worlds, in a place some called the Corridor of Doors and others called the Hall of Eternity, that something that should never have happened—happened. It began when the lights started to flicker off and on.

Then it stopped.

All seemed back to how it was supposed to be, except, it wasn't. There was enough time for a sigh of relief and to thank your God before one by one the lights went off, leaving a growing stretch of silence in the expanding darkness.

It was like the soldiers and sentries, each guarding and protecting their Door, had become blind in the all encompassing darkness and deaf in the silence.

Hardly any time passed, however, before their eyes were drawn to a small dot of light. Slowly the light stretched out into a thin sliver of silver that framed a door. It was a door beyond the imagination of most—a door that some claimed, with absolute certainty, had been welded shut by the heat of creation itself.

For in its long and ancient history, no door within the Corridor had ever opened without its Key. Wonderful and sad epic tales in poetry and prose had been written about fantastic and terrible worlds lost (legends really), of kings, queens, princes, paupers … of ancient lovers separated by worlds for all of eternity.

BOOM. The heavy door shifted. It held, but only for three beating heartbeats, and with its failure the forces of chaos and destruction were unleashed.

Freezing mist from a dying and decaying world spilled through the breach, bringing with it an unbearable stench and an oppressive sadness. Unfolding from the cold fog, a nightmarish creature advanced upon them like an avenging angel.

Concealed under a hooded cloak, its black robe flailing wildly in the turbulence, it walked the Corridor. Its sharp talons scratched and bit deeply into the polished, teal-veined marble floor.

Strewn and sinking to the cold hard floor, the soldiers and sentries had no recourse … unable to stop what was never supposed to happen from happening. One by one, they fell … leaving but one man standing.

A Knight, clad in armor of tarnished silver and gold, drew his great sword. He was mature, battle-scarred, and exquisitely muscled. His posture and stance left no doubt as to the great abilities that resided within him, qualities of strength and determination tempered by the experiences of too much war, too much death, and too much loss.

The closing space between them stilled.

"Impressive Gatekeeper," the Creature rasped.

Without fear, the Knight gazed into the black void of the Creature's hood, into the lenses of an ancient dark soul.

"Why have you come?" asked the Knight, struggling for breath.

"I have a message … for your Lady." From its breath ice crystals formed.

"Harbinger," said the Knight, "you shall not enter."

"So be it." Slowly it raised its arms, calling forth a power more cold and menacing than the blackness that surrounded them. Dark dense matter shrieked from the desolate world that had been unlocked.

Bracing for the onslaught of an evil gale, the Knight heard a distinctive click.

He turned.

Surrounded in a radiant golden light appeared the figure of a woman wearing a long flowing gown. In her hand, she held a Key on a finely woven gold and silver chain.

"Please," the woman spoke calmly, "accompany me." And she invited the Creature into her world.

The Knight, desiring to protect his Lady, wanted to object, but one look from her stately eyes made him acquiesce. He sheathed his sword.

With the Creature at her side, they entered the garden, which on any other day would have been filled with the sounds of life, birds in flight, and animals that stalked the ground on all fours. At this hour, the garden was unnaturally silent. In the open air, walking on the naked earth, the unusual qualities of the Creature could be seen, for with every step he took, flowers faded and leaves wilted, disintegrating at the softest touch of a breeze.

They arrived at the edge of a great stone fountain, from which streams of water flowed.

The Creature bowed deeply before her.

"Arise," she said, and kissed him on his pale cheek; she was one of the few living beings unaffected by his touch. "What news?" she asked in a somber voice.

As the Creature spoke, thick fog encircled them so that no one, by chance or by design, would see or hear their words.

"My Lady," his voice was dry and cold, "you know I attend to the dying."

She nodded.

"I found her against a shattered tree. About her were the fallen ... the remains of two great armies."

The Creature's voice changed, its pitch growing higher, becoming that of a female gasping for breath, *"My dear dear sister, I have failed."*

"Eupheme," the Lady looked into its ancient eyes, and saw the unspeakable horror that had transpired.

The Lady looked away. Her reflection in the fountain's water revealed the raw emotions of her pain and grief.

"They come," rasped the Harbinger, in his own voice. "Those thought dead have resurrected. Armies march against you."

The Lady, her face once again calm and serene, placed her hand on his arm and spoke softly, "Belothemus, my ally from the dark realm, will you grant me one wish?"

The Creature nodded. Had he known what she would ask of him, he would have wisely said no, but rightly or wrongly, he had already bound himself to her.

The Lady was gone for only a short time, returning with a bundle in her arms. The soft gray blanket hid what lay inside.

A small wonderful sound issued from its cocoon: It was the sound of a child, a baby girl, no more than a year old. Lovingly, the Lady caressed the child's pink cheek.

"Take my child," she said gravely. "If my Kingdom falls, the hopes of worlds will live with her."

Without fear, the beautiful child with blond hair and dazzling hazel eyes grinned as she grasped one of his great hands.

In a sweeping motion, the Harbinger swept the child into his arms, throwing his robe protectively about her as a sliver of light framed the mist.

"Hide her," said Lady Tiamore, her voice faltering, "Hide her so well that you, your people, and even God in his far away Heaven cannot find her."

CHAPTER 1

Strange and Unfamiliar Places

Khia Aleyne Ashworth fought her way back from a troubled sleep. Taking a deep breath in and a slow breath out, she tried to relax and tell herself that there was nothing to be frightened of, and that her dark and vivid dreams were mere fantasy. Except, she knew deep down inside that that wasn't true. Her dreams, more frequent and more disturbing, were trying to tell her something. Someone was moving Heaven and Earth looking for her … and they were getting closer.

At first she wasn't sure where she was. She had that feeling you get when you just wake up—that in-between place of not being asleep but not being awake either.

Slowly she looked around. She was in a small dark room. The curtains were closed. A silver sliver of pre-dawn light parted the curtains and filtered its way into the room. Everything seemed strange, yet somehow familiar.

Seven days, six nights … that's how long she'd been here—not nearly long enough for her to call it her own.

As she felt the late August breeze drift idly towards her, the light expanded. Khia shivered, but she wasn't cold. Sinking deeper into the warmth of her cocoon, she cuddled next to her seven-year-old brother, who was fast asleep. Khia nudged him gently. "Come on, Devon," she whispered in his ear. "It's time … it's time for you to go."

"Already?" a protesting, sleepy voice mumbled.

Devon had snuck into Khia's room some time past midnight. She knew his routine—knew that he'd wait until he was sure that everyone was asleep before he attempted the long dark and scary corridor. Khia timed his arrivals so that it had become a bit of a game. He'd run into her room and she'd expertly throw the covers up and over him in a graceful arc as he settled in beside her.

At daybreak, before anyone was awake, Devon would have to return to his room. With practiced stealth, they moved as quietly as church mice. The sounds of their whispered voices, the bed squeaking, their footsteps padding across the wooden floor, and the bedroom door creaking open were sounds that might have given them and their secret away, but no one stirred—not even the dog.

Tiptoeing down the corridor, Devon approached the dog, which was lying between him and his room.

Khia braced herself as she watched.

Fortunately, the Australian shepherd had long ago been habituated to children sneaking around the house, and merely lifted an eyebrow and one floppy ear. She wagged her docked tail a few times, stretched, and then pressed herself closer to the floor.

Finally Devon reached his room, but it seemed to have taken forever. He turned, waved to his sister, and yawned as he disappeared behind his door as if vanishing into another world.

With a soft click, Khia closed her door. Rather than returning to bed, she repositioned the white plastic chair by the window and opened the curtains. With her chin resting on her arms, she looked out and watched the sun break the horizon.

She was so scared of losing Devon. Here they were in yet another foster family, but for how long? And what about the next time?

The Brislings were okay, she supposed—just the latest family in a long line of people who had taken them in. Their previous placement had lasted two nights. Awakened by the sound of the telephone ringing, and a brief conversation in hushed tones, their things had been thrown into duffel bags and dumped onto the front porch, where they had been told to sit and wait.

Holding her sleepy brother in her arms, Khia hadn't known what to do, but it hadn't been long before a silver and gold sports car arrived in a blur of dust and wind. It was an expensive car, much too expensive for the salary of a social worker, but Khia hadn't thought of that at the time.

A dark-haired sophisticated woman, wearing a perfectly fitted black dress, high heels with red soles, and designer shades, stepped out of the car. Khia had felt shivers run through her as the woman walked towards them. Not bothering to remove her sunglasses, the tall slender woman introduced herself as Ms Percival, in a tone that had invited no questions or arguments. She had, however, explained that Mrs. McKinnon, their regular social worker, had had an unforeseen matter to attend to and that it was she who would be taking them to their new foster home.

After driving for what had seemed like hours, they had arrived at the Brislings: Pauline and Tom and their three daughters—Snowden, Morgan and Audrey. They were a church going family, dressed in their Sunday best. Having just returned from service, they looked like they could have been the poster family for the foster-care agency.

The three girls looked so pretty in their lovely dresses. Self-consciously, Khia twirled her long dark hair and looked down at her worn and faded jeans and old sneakers.

Mrs. Brisling was the first to greet them. She was a plain woman with gray eyes and dark blond hair. She had a tendency to talk too much, especially when she was nervous, and she had rattled on that day.

Spouting the ten rules of the house as though they were the Ten Commandments, Mrs. Brisling proceeded to give them the grand tour of the kitchen, the bathroom, and the den. Then she smiled and opened the next door. "And this, Devon, is your room."

Khia remembered having had to stifle a laugh at the look of horror on Devon's face when he saw the pink walls.

"Don't worry about the color, dear. When we have time we're going to paint it a color you want. Okay, sweetie?" Mrs. Brisling patted Devon's blond head.

The Brislings appeared to be a normal family, but Khia didn't think she was the best judge of such things. After all, what was normal? She'd been in too many foster homes to know. Sadly, what she had learned was that it didn't take long before the true characters of people and families were revealed. Right now they were in the introductory stage—the stage where they were special, because they were still new and vaguely interesting.

After the rules, the tour, and the quick cup of tea, it was time for Ms Percival to leave. Khia knew the routine; she'd experienced it many times before and was expecting the reassuring squeeze on the arm and the dreaded knowing smile. Khia wondered if such squeezes and smiles were meant for her or to make the social worker feel better.

Instead, Ms Percival surprised her when she whispered in her ear, "You'll be safe here."

She watched Ms Percival walking to her gold and silver car. Despite having known her for only a few hours, and not having had near enough time to form a proper opinion of her, she felt like she was being abandoned again. Her eyes burned, but she couldn't cry. She clung to her brother's hand and pushed down the urge to run.

In the end, did anything really matter? She'd never see Ms Percival again and knew (or thought she knew) what her and her brother's fate would be. For as soon as the reams of paperwork required by the system had been completed, once the army of social workers and their commanding officers of administrators, lawyers, and justices had followed their ponderously slow procedures, she and her brother would officially become wards of the state, and when she turned sixteen in a few months, they would take Devon away.

Khia shook her head, trying to rid herself of the memories of the past—memories of the accident that took her father's life, memories of her mother grieving and never able to accept his death ... and memories of being taken away.

If only they'd had one more chance ... if only ...

Khia stared out the bedroom window and watched the sunrise. She noticed a black bird perched on a streetlight with its head cocked to one side. It seemed to be looking right at her.

"Khiaaa. Khiaaa," it cawed loudly, and launched itself into the air, flapped its wings, and disappeared.

CHAPTER 2

Poor Old Meg

... and so it begins.

Khia placed her empty glass on the counter. "Would you like some help, Mrs. Brisling?"

Khia had noticed that Morgan and Snowden followed a predictable pattern. The two girls appeared promptly for meals but quickly disappeared when it came time for the washing up.

"Honey," said Mrs. Brisling, looking at Khia, "there's no need."

"Please, I'd like to help."

"You're such a sweet child," said Mrs. Brisling.

While Mrs. Brisling rattled on about nothing in particular, Khia smiled shyly. Despite her best efforts, she found herself tuning out, and focused her attention on Audrey and Devon, who were absorbed in a robust fantasy world of their own creation. Arrayed about them, propped up everywhere, were their plush animals, dolls, and toys.

Drying the last glass and placing it on the top shelf, Mrs. Brisling asked Khia, "Do you want to come to the city with Audrey and me?"

"Huh?"

"The city," she repeated. "Do you want to come with Audrey and me to the city?"

Khia's transparent smile gave it away.

Khia and Devon had lived near the city core three (or perhaps it was four) families ago. Khia liked going downtown; she found it a fascinating place, with all kinds of interesting things to see and do. One of the things Khia loved was watching people, and to her, the city was like an ocean tide that filled and emptied every morning and every night.

Buckled in the aging family minivan, Khia sat quietly in the front seat, listening to the radio.

"Wuuwee!" the commentator's voice boomed over the radio. "It's gonna be another scorcher! Got an extreme weather alert with temperatures above 101 ... might break a record! UV readings are high so wear your sunscreen kids. It's going to last a couple of more days ... maybe the rest of the week. And now, the news ..."

Mrs. Brisling turned off the radio. As they drove through the rolling hills, she softly hummed an old jingle from a long-dead advertisement that had lured people to the area. "The ideal place to bring up the perfect middle-class family," she laughed, but there was an edge to it. "The civilized and the wild."

It was almost as if Mrs. Brisling wanted to get away just as much as Khia did.

"How long have you lived here?" asked Khia.

"I've lived in the suburbs all of my life." She proceeded to give Khia the condensed history of the White Hills, which were situated between the mountains to the west, the grassy flat plains to the east, and the hot desert to the south.

The car glided onto one of the feeder lanes and it wasn't long before they were shunted onto the interstate. Traffic, as always, was congested and it took them longer than expected to get to the city center's core. Late for their appointment, Mrs. Brisling parked the car in an underground parking garage. Complaining of its excessive price, she inserted her credit card, and as if by magic, the arm rose up and allowed them entry.

In a sparkling clean reception area, Audrey clung to her mother's hand as they were whisked into the doctor's office. Khia, seeing her chance, grabbed Devon's hand and they swept themselves towards the door, which swooshed open for them as if on cue.

Not really knowing where they were going, Khia and Devon set off on their own course, with their eyes heavenward, looking at the great buildings that seemed to merge with the very sky itself.

Khia loved it. She felt free. They walked, gawked, and looked at all the things for sale through clean glass windows—all of it so tantalizingly near but so frustratingly far.

Sitting on a concrete barrier, surrounded by glass and steel, they let the city flow beside them just as if they were on a shoreline, except they were on a busy square near the entrance of a large downtown mall. Several bright LED billboards advertised luxury cars, expensive perfumes, and designer clothes in an endlessly repeating cycle of color, flashing logos, and movement. Not far from them, a policeman was directing traffic— one lane was blocked due to a broken water main. Khia watched as water, like a small river, flowed onto the road.

Sounds drew Khia's eyes to opposite corners of the square; a busker played a drum on one corner, and a shabbily dressed bag lady paced back and forth on the other, holding a staff in one hand and a sign in the other—written in shaky red letters that warned anyone who bothered to read them that '*the end is nigh*'.

It seemed like the busker and the bag lady were in a competition, vying for coins and the attention of the pedestrians that streamed endlessly past. But, in an odd juxtaposition, it also seemed like they were working in a kind of magical tandem; the dynamic sounds of the square complimented what each was doing, as though they were lead characters on a briskly moving stage.

The drummer kept a lively rhythm and his hat was filling with coins. In contrast, the homeless woman was shunned. She looked old and frail, but she spoke in a surprisingly loud and clear voice. She had found a sweet spot, a focal point, and her voice, interwoven with the drum beat, echoed across the square, gathering its own momentum; it reverberated against the surrounding skyscrapers and warned that a great flood would devastate the earth.

Khia leaned over to her brother, and because the square was full of sound and movement, she spoke loudly. "The world would never be destroyed that way again. After the great flood there was a rainbow and …"

In that very moment, as Khia spoke those seemingly innocent words, an extraordinary and most unexpected thing happened. A sudden lull—a silencing gap—filled the square and disturbed the flow of sound like a discordant off-note key in a well-rehearsed orchestra. Khia's words had set off something nameless.

The drummer faltered in his complex rhythm. Curiously, he looked up for a split second but just as quickly resumed his play, catching up to where he should have been, almost as if he'd never missed a beat. However, in that missed beat, two cars collided, causing confusion and disorder. The traffic cop shook his head and moved towards the tangle of cars, blaring horns, angry voices, and in the distance, the sounds of sirens.

No one in the square could pinpoint what, or who, had caused the disharmony, except for Khia, Devon … and one other.

The bag lady stopped her warnings and lamentations, with a look of consternation on her face. Intently, she stared at Khia and Devon as if they were the only two people on the busy square, but then she suddenly became distracted, and looked up into the shadows of the towering buildings.

Khia looked where the old woman was looking, and for a moment, she too saw something—something unidentifiable that chilled her and made her blood run cold. Whatever it was clung to the shadows and crawled towards them, vague ripples in the places where there was an absence of light.

Khia held her breath. It approached closer, and closer … skittering like a fluttering bat.

And pounced.

The bag lady jerked backwards, horror fixed on her face. With one gnarled hand, she gripped her staff tightly while her other loosened and the sign toppled over, ever so slowly, and struck the ground.

Something had taken possession of her; her eyes, not her own, had turned wild and dangerous.

As if in a fog, the bag lady gathered her worldly possessions, (the contents of her grocery cart and her precious staff) and pushed her old grocery cart awkwardly across the street making her way towards Khia and Devon. She was no more than halfway through the intersection when the traffic lights changed. Impatient drivers honked their horns, made obscene gestures with their hands, and yelled at her to get out of the way. In response, she muttered incoherent invectives, all the while intently staring at Khia.

Khia and Devon wanted to flee, but their feet seemed stuck; it was like an invisible force was keeping them in place. All Khia could hear was the screech of the old, damaged grocery cart coming closer and closer.

She stopped only a few inches from them.

The old hag's face was creased, and her angry eyes were puffy discolored bags of yellow and purple. One eye looked infected, blood shot, and crisscrossed with angry streaks of red. With one hand, she brushed her unkempt filthy hair. It was an almost feminine gesture, an unconscious memory of years past when she was young, and perhaps beautiful, and when such an action would have drawn attention to her appearance, rather than revulsion.

"Hello … little brats … little demons," the bag lady spat. "Did you think I would not notice you for who you are?" She laughed menacingly, slurring her words. "You've come to torment poor old Meg, again?"

"Uh lady," Khia answered, "we … uh … we have to go." Khia grabbed Devon's hand and wrenched her feet into action.

"Demons. Demons!" the bag lady screamed at them, but they didn't stop running until the sounds of the drum had faded away.

CHAPTER 3

Dodger and Goula

Tipping point.

Khia stopped.

They had run into an alley. Thinking it would lead them to the streets beyond, it had fooled them. Instead it had turned into a blind dead end.

What to do? Turn around. Wait.

They waited.

Enough time had passed to catch their breath, when Khia and Devon looked at each other. Relieved, they laughed nervously at their misadventure. Then they heard the unmistakable sound of a screeching grocery cart.

The bag lady made her way closer; a shadow darkened the alley.

Khia braced herself.

"Devil children. Devil children. Devil children," the bag lady repeated, as if it was some kind of a hypnotic mantra. "Did you think you could escape me? No … no … NO," she cackled, waving her staff at them, a wicked hungry smile on her face.

"Time for me to send you back, back to your cages, into the earth where you belong. Back to your stench. Back to your pit!" she screamed. "And then you won't never bother old Meg again. Yes … Out of Meg's old head …Yes … no!" Meg cried out, placing a grimy hand to her temple, trying to force whatever it was—the thing—from her head. Her eyes took on a glass-like quality. Her smile widened, revealing blackened rotting teeth.

Backing up, Khia watched in amazement as the bag lady stooped down and picked up a cigarette butt off the ground. From her half-torn pocket, she took out a crumpled book of matches, cupped her grimy hands to protect the flame, lit the stub, and sucked in deeply, savoring the moment. The gray smoke from her extinguished match and the smoldering tobacco circled around her, making her look larger and more menacing … like casting shadows on the wall.

The bag lady stepped away from her cart and approached Khia and Devon. Coughing, she threw the cigarette butt away and leaned heavily on her staff. Gathering fluids from deep in her throat, she spat blood and thick black phlegm. The viscous sickly fluid struck the pavement near their feet. Khia suppressed a gag.

The bag lady slowly straightened her spine, and audible cracks were heard. With a dirty sleeve, she casually wiped blood and spittle from her mouth and refocused her attention on Khia and Devon.

Grabbing Devon, Khia tried to make a run for it, but there was nowhere to run. The bag lady blocked their path, and behind them was a solid brick wall.

"Oh you can't escape," she jeered. Gripping her staff, she corralled them as a shepherd might herd his flock, forcing them back, step by step, until their backs bumped up against the wall.

To her left, Khia spotted a door that she hadn't noticed before, and felt there might yet be hope for an escape. She motioned to Devon. He scrambled over and fumbled with the knob, but it wouldn't budge.

Instinctively protecting Devon, Khia stepped in front of him. Defiantly, knowing it was better to look directly at her fate, she stood straight, fists clenched at her side, trying very hard to stop her knees from shaking.

The bag lady sneered at her cruelly, giving her indictment, "Devil child. Devil child."

She raised her staff high above her head, preparing to strike.

Khia's mind raced. She was thinking about Devon, thinking about what she could do, thinking about why they had run from Mrs. Brisling, and why they had entered the alley. She felt an incredible anger well up inside her, and as though it were really happening, she foresaw the painful killing blow.

And in that moment, time slowed. Somewhere above, Khia heard a bird caw loudly, "Khiaaa. Khiaaa."

Unexpectedly, the locked door, which Devon had tried so desperately to open, opened, and a black man and white woman stepped into the alley, engrossed in an animated conversation.

"Hello! What's going on here?" the black man said, with an Irish lilt.

Expressions of fear and horror etched on their faces, as Meg's wooden staff began its punishing decent …

Like lightning, the black man sprinted forward. He grabbed hold of the staff and absorbed as much of its downward energy as he could, but he could not absorb it all.

Lower and lower the staff descended. The blow made contact with Khia, but instead of a killing blow, it merely touched her shoulder as lightly as if she were being knighted.

The bag lady seethed. Khia was speechless. Devon heaved a huge sigh of relief.

There was a loud crack, a flash that was almost too fast to see, and something nameless shrieked and was gone.

"Would you hurt these young ones?" the black Irishman spoke loudly, a few inches from Meg's contorted face.

As if coming out of a dream, Meg slowly became aware of the two strangers who stood between her and her prey. She blinked, trying to clear her eyes.

"Good woman!" His voice was softer now, filled with empathy now that the danger had passed.

A growing spark of sanity returned to Meg's eyes. Confused, unsure of how or why she was in the alley, she looked at Khia and Devon.

Ashamed, Meg loosened her grip on her staff, which slipped from her dirty trembling fingers and fell to the ground.

With the mesmerizing black man before her, Meg finally managed to speak, her stuttering words sounding timid and frightened. "Y-yes … yes … I-I …" Meg shook her head aimlessly from side to side, and they could see that she was troubled.

"Dear heart," spoke the black man's companion, who stepped forward with a handful of bills. "Take these," she said gently and took Meg's filthy hand, placing the bills into them.

The act of kindness pierced Meg, hurting her more than shouting or being struck ever could. She lowered her head; her greasy gray hair partially covered her eyes and face, and for a moment Khia saw her as a young and beautiful woman.

The moment was broken; clutching the bills, Meg turned and tottered away, leaving her staff and grocery cart behind.

The fair-skinned woman with the penetrating blue eyes turned towards Khia, "Now what in Saint Patrick's name did you do to attract this kind of attention?"

She waited patiently for an answer, but Khia had none to give.

It was the black Irishman who spoke. "Ah Goula, the children aren't at fault; this is the work of Ez—"

Stopping his thought mid-word, the beautiful lady arched one of her eyebrows in a silent and unmistakable look of disapproval.

"Ah … yes, well … no matter. Ah … the name's Dodger," he bowed gallantly. "And this fine woman," he said, with a graceful sweep of his arm, "is Goula."

Goula smiled, "And what would your names be?"

Although Khia remained guarded, Devon was utterly transfixed. "Hello," he said. "My name's Devon Ashworth and this is my sister Khia. I'm seven."

Khia scowled at her brother and he said no more.

"It's a pleasure to meet you Devon and Khia." Goula spoke casually, as if she hadn't noticed Khia's scowl and Devon's silence, "Come, let us escort you from this dark passage."

Before they walked out of the alley, Goula picked up Meg's staff and leaned it up against the wall, where a single sliver of light broke the shadows. "Poor old soul, I imagine she'll come back for it."

"Let's get you home. But how about a soft drink?" Dodger asked in an animated voice "And a sausage? You know, when I'm in America, I do love a sausage on a bun. Not a hot dog mind but a proper sausage …"

Their voices faded from the alley, leaving Meg's staff and grocery cart in the lightly swirling dust and litter.

†

Not long afterwards, a woman with steel gray eyes, accompanied by a young girl of sixteen, entered the empty alley.

"What have you learned here, Katrina?" asked the steely-eyed woman.

"Nothing of interest. An old staff, a grocery cart filled with junk."

"Look again," was the older woman's harsh response.

Katrina, frustrated by the question, remained silent.

"With experience you'll see patterns, patterns that fit and ones that don't. With time you will learn how to bring them to the surface. Listen for secrets. Whispers."

Before the formidable woman could say any more, two large muscular men with cropped hair, dressed in expensive, tailor-made suits, approached. No matter how well dressed they were, the twins, Burdock and Cocklebur, could not conceal their bulk and intimidating presence. They were a pair you would never want to cross paths with—especially down a dark dead-end alley.

"Lady Ezrulie," said Burdock, the older by five minutes and perhaps the wiser of the two, "we have secured images for you." He gave Ezrulie a pleased smile of success as he handed her a grainy photograph, which had been enhanced, of a boy and girl. "It shouldn't take long before we find out where they live."

"Major Burdock, keep me informed," the older woman answered, with a smile that made a man who was afraid of nothing shiver.

Burdock bowed, about to turn and leave.

"Oh, Major," Ezrulie paused, "there is one more thing you can do for me. Open that door." She motioned towards the door—the very same door that Dodger and Goula had used to enter the alley.

Burdock gestured to his brother. Cocklebur, flexing his large biceps, went to the door and turned the knob. Metal snapped in his large hand and clanged to the ground as the door swung open.

"Bricked-up space," he announced.

"A door that leads to nowhere," grumbled Burdock, for his brother.

Angrily, Ezrulie spat, "They had help. The two had help."

She called the young girl, who was disdainfully sifting through Meg's belongings. "Katrina," said Ezrulie sharply. "What do you notice about the door?"

Katrina looked up and answered, "It's all bricked up."

"Anything else?" asked Ezrulie.

Katrina shook her head, "No."

"Look again," said Ezrulie impatiently

Katrina approached and touched the brick wall. "The bricks are warm, yet they rest in shadow. A conduit? Is it possible?" She smiled with interest. "A Portal."

"What else do you see?" asked Ezrulie.

Katrina scanned the alleyway but saw nothing.

Ezrulie's gaze directed Katrina to something that lay in the alley. Devon's baseball cap, the one he had carelessly stuffed into his pocket earlier that day, lay in the wind-blown litter.

"Pity we have nothing of the girl's, but this will do," Ezrulie said, as she placed the baseball cap into a clear plastic bag that she carefully sealed.

"There is nothing more for us here," declared Ezrulie.

The young girl was suddenly elated; her lesson for the day was over. She roughly pushed Meg's grocery cart, causing it to tip over and the assortment of Meg's possessions to spill out. The screeching sound stopped when the bad wheel stopped turning. Walking over to Meg's staff, which Goula had propped up against the wall, Katrina gave it a sharp kick, neatly breaking it in two. The pieces fell to the ground, one landing in the last vestiges of light and the other in shade.

Younger than her years, Katrina skipped out of the alley like an innocent little girl and got into a large black car with dark-tinted windows.

CHAPTER 4

Pond

In your neighborhood...

Khia felt the dry wind on her face as she followed Snowden down the White Hills on a clunky old bike.

Devon, pedaling faster and faster, tried to keep up. Leaving the paved road, Snowden led them to a narrow dirt path, which ended at a steep eroded edge that was held together by a few scraggy bushes and stunted grasses.

Discarding the bikes, Khia looked over the edge. She didn't like the look of this place; it gave her the creeps, but before she could say anything, Devon had already followed Snowden down the steep slope kicking up great dust clouds and pushing down waves of sandy earth until they reached the bottom.

"Come on," motioned Snowden impatiently. "It's this way." She trotted along the path, disappearing into a dense copse of trees.

For the past few days, Khia had been feeling increasingly apprehensive; it was like a storm was building but hadn't yet broken.

Shaking her head, she followed her brother and Snowden under the canopy. The change couldn't have been more abrupt, and indeed they had entered a different world—a humid world of shadow, where light barely filtered through. The occasional fleeting beam of sunlight felt like searchlights moving lazily about ... searching for them. She shivered.

Deeper and deeper they ventured into the woods. Old gnarled trees supported a profusion of green mosses and ivy creepers, which leapt up as if trying to wrestle them to the ground. A small clearing brought them to a stagnant pond where algae grew rampant on the surface of the water.

The pond was at most twenty feet in diameter. An unimpressive concrete dam (whose foundation had long ago cracked and eroded) held back the water. A trickle of water flowed into a culvert with steel reinforcement bars that were rusted and twisted.

Snowden ran down to the concrete dam and sat down with her legs dangling over the edge, with her feet just inches above the brackish water.

"Well, what do you think?" asked Snowden, totally ignoring Devon but trying to impress Khia, who was a year older.

"It's interesting," Khia replied evasively, but the pond gave her the creeps. There was something she didn't like about it.

Snowden dug into her shirt pocket and pulled out a small clear plastic bag. Inside were three cigarettes that she delicately handled, as if they were gold. She took one and held it between her lips.

"Want one?" she asked, in tone that she thought made her sound older, and more mature.

Khia shook her head.

Imitating her father, Snowden pulled out a book of matches and lit one, but the match blew out. Pulling out another mostly used book of matches, she made two more attempts and a rush of burnt fuel flared up. She brought the flame towards the cigarette that she held between her lips. Closing one eye, she placed the burning match at the end of the cigarette and inhaled. The cigarette glowed, and smoke twirled. Tossing the spent match, Khia watched as it sailed through the air like a missile, and into the pond where it went out with an angry hiss.

"How about a drag?" Snowden asked in a conspiratorial voice, scooting closer to where Khia sat, holding out the cigarette.

"No thanks," replied Khia.

"Suit yourself." Snowden brought the cigarette to her lips and inhaled deeply. Suppressing a cough, she quickly exhaled a puff of gray smoke.

Khia thought Snowden looked really silly with a cigarette dangling from her mouth. She watched two streams of smoke come off the end of the cigarette—one blue, the other an ashy gray. The smoke rose up and curled around in the slow moving air, merging into a chaotic homogenized heap that floated about like a small dirty cloud.

Three silent seconds passed.

Snowden took another drag, but this time was unable to hold back a cough.

Finishing her cigarette, she crushed the butt, tossed it into the pond, and an unnatural hush fell upon them.

"What was that?" whispered Devon startled.

All three felt it. All three stood very, very still. Listening.

Khia shrugged her shoulders as if it was nothing.

High above, a small gray cloud moved in front of the sun, and their surroundings fell into shadow. The pond took on a sinister, cauldron-like quality, making it look like some kind of a radioactive reservoir ready to bubble over.

The air was thick. It was as if the smoke from Snowden's cigarette had expanded into a pall of gray over the pond. Khia heard (or thought she heard) faint female voices chanting. It was as if a coven of far-away witches were casting a spell. The eerie sounds swirled like a vortex and Khia imagined something stirring underneath the putrid water, coming for them … coming out of its deep dark hole.

An urgent caw sounded above their heads, "Khiaaaa. Khiaaa."

They ran.

Devon stumbled and fell. Khia skidded to a stop to help, but Snowden kept going, disappearing from view.

Khia heard leaves rustling, branches snapping, and a deep growl. The shape of a huge silver-gray wolf emerged—all teeth and fangs and fur. The creature bounded towards them. Khia grabbed Devon and crouched down, using her body to shield him, with her fists tightly clenched. Horrified, Khia braced herself, but the wolf bounded up and over them. Snarling, it headed towards the screeching black bird that was circling above and diving at the putrid pond.

Khia felt anger bubble within her, and an inexplicable urge to fight; it welled up inside her: a euphoric desire to join the silver wolf and the black bird.

Devon touched her hand. And the feeling disappeared.

They fled.

Behind them, they heard distorted and chaotic sounds. The sound could have been anything: the pathetic cry of a bird whose wing was broken, floundering in circles on the blue-green algae; the silver-gray wolf, its forelegs snapped, its snout sinking into the murky slimy water; or perhaps the throttled sounds of a monster being driven back into its deep dark hole.

Huffing and puffing, and out of breath, Khia and Devon reached the edge of the trees. Coming out of the shadows, the full shock of the hot sun struck them. Sweating, they reached the steep sandy incline and began their ascent.

Snowden had already reached the safety of the ridge. It was a hard climb. It seemed for every three steps up, they slid down two—frantically clawing their way up, pulling out tufts of dried plants, and pushing down great heaps of dry earth.

Khia helped Devon heave himself up over the ledge. He flopped down on the ground. His face was dusty and dirty, and he held his side—the pain from the stitch was almost unbearable.

Khia and Snowden looked over the edge, trying to see what it was that had terrified them so.

"What was it?" asked Snowden.

Absolutely nothing moved below, not even the rustling of leaves. Khia felt the unease. It was as if there was something below, looking up, watching, and waiting.

"Nothing," said Khia, realizing that Snowden hadn't seen anything. "Just our imaginations."

Her brother looked up at her and didn't say a word.

Snowden laughed as if it were the funniest thing that had ever happened, "Wow! You guys were so scared!" After a few long moments, and still laughing, she announced, "It's time to go home. Don't want to be late for lunch." Then, in her best John Wayne accent, she said, "Mount up; we roll." She had copied that from old movies her parents had made her watch.

Khia reached out and pulled Devon to his feet. "Come on, it's all uphill now," she said, as she glanced back into the shadowy glen.

They jumped up onto their bikes and the three of them started the difficult trek. Snowden, true to her character, cycled ahead, putting more and more distance between them until she was lost from sight.

"You all right?" Khia asked Devon, but he was still holding his side.

"We'll walk," suggested Khia, and they got off their bikes. It had been much more fun riding down the hill.

†

At a slow pace, Khia and Devon made their way towards their guardians' house. It was high noon and they were late for lunch. It was the hottest part of the day and no one was on the street. The neighborhood was quiet and deserted, until a black car with tinted windows slowly passed.

The first time the car passed, Khia had barely noticed. Its reappearance, a couple of minutes later, attracted her attention, especially when it stopped a few hundred feet ahead, with its engine left idling.

Odd, thought Khia, issuing instructions to her brother.

Devon nodded; he understood what they had to do.

As nonchalantly as possible, feeling anything but calm, Khia (keeping her head rigidly straight) tried to see who was inside the car with just the corners of her eyes, but the tinted glass was impervious to her gaze.

She heard a soft click. Before the car door opened, she yelled, "Now!"

With almost supernatural vigor, they jumped onto their bikes and cycled as fast as they could. When they were a few hundred feet from the Brislings, Khia passed Devon, rode straight up the driveway into the garage, and jumped off her bike, which went crashing into the corner. As Devon came skidding in, she hit the automatic garage door console. The garage door closed like a castle's portcullis, protecting them from the outside world.

†

Burdock and Cocklebur entered Ezrulie's lavish penthouse apartment. Winding their way between the opulent furniture, they passed Katrina playing with a doll on the plush carpet.

"Isn't she a little old for that?" muttered Burdock.

Cocklebur shrugged. He didn't care.

They walked out and onto a large balcony that had been manicured into a stunning sanctuary. Ezrulie stood with her back to them, her hands splayed across the edge of a leaded glass barrier, looking at the panoramic view of the city. The sun was setting. A moderately strong wind whistled around her, blowing beads of water from a gold and silver fountain that featured two warring figures, locked in perpetual conflict. Behind her, a pasty-faced man dressed in a nondescript suit stood, gripping his briefcase.

Ezrulie had felt their presence before their feet had touched the elevator in the P1 level of the underground parking area, seventy-two floors below, and she knew that they had failed in achieving their objectives. She turned towards them.

"Your presence distresses me." She shook her head, looking at the men's disarray. Burdock and Cocklebur had various cuts and scrapes that had been haphazardly attended to.

Ezrulie paused, letting the tension rise. "You let the girl get away. What am I ... to do ... with such incompetence?"

Burdock stepped forward. "My Lady," he bowed in deference before her. "We found them; we know where they live, but unforeseen circumstances have arisen."

"Complications, Major?" Her eyebrows arched accusingly.

"They are protected," he answered.

"I trust, gentlemen," she paused, "that you know the cost of failure?"

As Burdock and Cocklebur departed, Ezrulie turned her attention to the man gripping his briefcase. "Mr. Elliot," she said.

Mr. Elliot carefully placed his briefcase on the glass table. With visibly shaking hands, he inserted a silver key into its slot and the case clicked opened.

CHAPTER 5

Father Tobias

Thus the heavens and the earth were com-
pleted in all their vast array. Genesis 2:1

On the seventh day, Mr. Brisling hoped to smoke and lounge away the day, but his wife had different plans. She had a list of *honey-do jobs*. Being a fair man, Mr. Brisling delegated most of his chores to the kids.

By dinnertime, Mr. Brisling was at the barbecue, cooking juicy sizzling burgers, while Mrs. Brisling had prepared baked potatoes with sour cream and chives, and a green garden salad with red plump tomatoes. She was just finishing off dessert—a colorful fruit salad with whipped cream, complete with chocolate sauce drizzled on top—when Mr. Brisling announced, "Burgers are ready."

They had no sooner started to eat when it started to rain. After the long drought and hot temperatures, the rain was welcome. Under the canopy, they watched it fall gloriously from the sky.

†

Late that night, Khia lay in bed, listening to the sound of the rain, and drifted off to sleep ...

She stood high upon the ruins of a great bridge and looked down on a blackened, blasted wasteland. Immense marks scarred the earth. The remains of beasts, grotesque creatures, lay scattered amongst a multitude of fallen warriors, men and (by the shape of much of the armor) women who had fought and died in battle.

Khia was horrified by the scale of destruction. It was a scene that spanned the landscape. The final cataclysmic confrontation had poisoned the plain, making it unable to sustain or nurture life. Anyone who lingered too long in this abysmal place would surely sicken and die.

A small breeze caused the dry earth to swirl and the scene began to change. It was like watching a film in rewind, as the images sped backwards in time until it stopped.

The bridge shone golden in the fading sunset. Grand and majestic, it led to a beautiful city in the sky—a city of brilliant light.

And then she saw what looked like a small dot in the distance. As it neared, it seemed to transform into a darkened shadow of tens of thousands ... breaching the bridge.

Khia gasped. The bridge no longer shone golden. The black tide swept past, charging into the city, and began to lay waste to it, desecrating it with every step. No longer able to defend their city, she saw and felt the hopelessness and despair of its people as they fought to the death.

Like hearing its final breath, the bridge creaked and groaned. A fine crack emerged and stretched from one end to the other. The fault line deepened and the fissures fanned out like the branches of a tree. Ash from the burning city flew up into the sky and fell back to the earth like snow, and not being able to bear anymore weight, the bridge collapsed ... and the city fell from its dizzying height.

†

Khia woke up late. It was Sunday and they would be going to church. She set her feet weakly onto the floor and realized that her brother was not at her side. Her brother had been secretly sneaking into her bed for the longest time. Perhaps the rain had lulled him into sleep last night.

After a quick shower that turned cold, Khia put on her only dress; it was white and frilly. Khia liked to dress up, and when she looked in the mirror, she thought she looked rather nice—that was until she saw the three Brisling girls in their pretty dresses. Her white dress, she realized, wasn't white at all; it was more of a grayish color. Sadly, she slumped on the step not saying much of anything.

A few moments later, Devon (who was the last one to arrive) distracted Khia from her thoughts. He was dressed in a smart-looking, blue polyester suit with a clip on tie and black shoes, and had combed his hair, which he'd slicked back with water. *He looks really cute*, she thought, and her heart melted when she felt his small hand slip into hers.

†

St. Anne's Catholic Church was a few miles away, in the nearby town of Woburn. St. Anne's was one of the older churches in the area, having been founded officially in the 1880s, but its origins went back several more decades to the early settlements in the region. A large steeple guided churchgoers through Woburn's maze of old twisting roads and dead-end streets.

They pulled into the parking lot and walked to the church doors, where Father Tobias waited.

Father Tobias was a striking Italian, just under six feet, with black hair, olive skin, and warm brown eyes. At the parish for only a few months, he had taken note of the dwindling and aging congregation and made Herculean efforts to entice younger people back into the pews.

The priest greeted Mr. and Mrs. Brisling, shook their hands vigorously, and smiled at the children as they walked in.

Sitting in the third row, Devon started fidgeting and couldn't wait to go outside and play. Mass was so boring. He turned around and saw a big clock at the back of the church, and looked frequently at it to see if its hands had moved. At one point, he was convinced that the clock must have stopped, but the slow seconds ticked by and the minutes crawled. During the sermon, Devon shuffled his feet and played with the books set in front of him. He tried his best to stop his yawns but couldn't.

It was penance to suffer through the hour-long service. Would it never end? Everyone stood, and for a moment, Devon thought mass was over, but everyone started reciting the 'Our Father'. Devon had memorized most of the prayer and only stumbled a little at the end. When the prayer was over, he sat down like all the other worshipers. He copied the congregation: kneeling, standing, sitting. And just when he thought he had it all figured out, he stood, wanting to be the first one standing, but everyone knelt instead. It was a mystery to him.

In contrast, Khia was rather impressed and listened to every word. Father Tobias' homily was full of fire and brimstone; he was a powerful orator and very persuasive.

He described the battle of Heaven as if he had been there himself and was reliving a memory; he talked about the most beautiful and eldest of angels as if he'd seen him with his very own eyes. In vivid detail, he explained their vain attempt to usurp the glory and power of God ... and when victory seemed assured, the defenders of Heaven were pushed back to their gates, and found the courage and the fortitude to turn against the tide. Angels were cast down into eternal damnation, while the vaults of Hell closed.

†

Mass was finally over. Eager to run out and play, Devon found himself trapped. This time, he was forced to wait for the slow procession of the priest, deacons, and altar boys to wend their way to the front doors. The doors to the outside world seemed so far away, and to make matters worse, Father Tobias stood at the doorway where his practitioners crowded around him, slowing the exodus even more.

It seemed like an eternity. Devon was almost at the door, ready to bolt free, when he was again waylaid and forced to shake hands or have his hair tussled by people he didn't know. Khia dreaded it too but knew it was inevitable. The Brislings, standing at the top of the steps, were showered with accolades about how good they were to take in two unfortunate children.

Devon had finally been excused and ran out. Khia watched as he made his way into the graveyard and stopped in front of a weathered white statue of an angel with outstretched wings. She would have preferred to join her brother, but she stayed and smiled until her jaw hurt.

Eventually Khia reached the last step, and was about to join her brother when Father Tobias turned to her.

"How do you like staying at the Brislings?" asked the Priest pleasantly. "I imagine that such a full household must take getting used to." He smiled gently.

Khia nodded.

"It must be hard for you and your brother, but I can see that you are strong."

Khia glanced over at Devon and tensed when she realized that he was not alone. Devon was talking to a large muscular man with short-cropped hair; the man rested his hand on a black tombstone.

"I knew your mother," said the Priest.

That got her attention!

"I knew her before you were born ... before the terrible car accident."

Father Tobias knew our mother? How?

"She was a wonderful woman. Full of life," continued Father Tobias. As he placed a comforting hand on her shoulder, a terrific explosion blasted the basement windows out of the church, violently throwing the great oak doors open, and wrenching one of them from its iron moorings. Flames shot through the air.

Cast off the steps of the church, Father Tobias and Khia landed prostrate on the ground. Before Khia could even move, the priest was on his knees, shielding her with his body.

"Are you hurt?" he asked, with concern.

"I'm okay," she replied.

And with what looked like calm fear in his eyes, he said, "Your brother ... where is your brother?"

Her thoughts screamed. *Oh my God, Devon!*

"In the graveyard," she whispered.

"Go to him," the priest commanded, as he sprang into action.

Mesmerized, Khia watched his dark vestments swirl as Father Tobias turned and ran up the stone steps of the church, plunging into the billowing smoke. Oxygen and cold air created a pocket for him to enter, and he disappeared down the angular stairway into the church basement. The flames, it seemed, gathered energy as if to do battle with him.

The parishioners sprang into action and panic. Wailing and lamenting cries could be heard. Everyone seemed to be babbling at once—incomprehensible voices asking if everyone had gotten out, if anyone was hurt, and if anyone had called 911.

Another blast shook the church, shattering stained-glass windows; a mosaic of colors flew through the air and scattered to the ground.

The haunting words of the priest reverberated, penetrated into Khia's mind. *Devon!*

Khia wrenched her eyes away from the burning church, looking frantically for her brother. In the escalating confusion, she had seen him for a brief moment by the tombstones.

DEVON! She watched in horror. The large man with cropped hair had a firm hold on Devon's hand, and was leading him towards a large black car with tinted windows.

Khia ran, but people were in her way and they were agonizingly slow to move. It felt to her like the wind had suddenly kicked up and become thick and overpoweringly strong, as if actively trying to hinder her pursuit. She ran and yet it seemed as if she wasn't getting any closer. It felt like being in one of her bad dreams.

Khia's entire attention focused on her brother, being led away by the stranger. "Devon!" Khia screamed, but she was still too far away; her throat was dry, and her panicked voice didn't have weight.

The car door opened and she watched as Devon slipped in and disappeared behind metal and opaque glass.

"No!" she screamed.

No one heard—their attention held by the holocaust of their burning church.

Her very worst fears gripped her and Khia redoubled her efforts to reach her brother.

Out of breath, Khia reached the car and banged her fist hard on the dark glass. She was half expecting the car to drive away, leaving her in the dust and never seeing her brother again, but the door burst open.

"Ms Percival!" Khia gasped.

"Get in," the woman spoke sharply.

The back door opened and Khia got in. There was no way she was leaving her brother.

And the door slammed shut. She felt trapped.

As the car skidded away, Khia looked back and saw Mrs. Brisling, standing like a pillar near the burning church. Discretely, Mrs. Brisling raised one hand to her chest, a great sadness in her eyes as she watched them drive away.

Before they rounded the corner, the last thing Khia saw was Father Tobias. Silhouetted by angry red flames and black smoke, he staggered out of the church with an unconscious body in his arms. Coughing and covered in ash, he looked skywards and Khia thought he looked like an angel.

CHAPTER 6

Norbert and McBride

Khia shivered. She was scared and angry, but Devon, who was also trapped in a car with Ms Percival and two strange men, didn't seem to have a care in the world.

The large muscular man, who had led Devon away from the church graveyard, looked menacing with a jagged scar on his left cheek. The other man, the driver with the bald shiny head, turned, gave Khia a big smile, and winked at her.

Khia glanced questioningly at Ms Percival but got no reaction.

"Sorry girlie, if we gave you a scare back there!" said the bald man. "It's not every day we get to drive away with a brother and sister from a burning church. Although there *was* that time, remember Norbert," he rambled, "with those two young ladies from Soho, and the one who accidentally set that fire. Now those two were a lot of fun. The hard part was getting them back to where we found 'em without getting caught. I tell you there was hell to pay ..."

Norbert, who was sitting in the back seat with Khia and Devon, coughed loudly. Leaning forward, he gave his friend a nudge. "Not the right time, McBride," he said firmly. "We'll have plenty of time to tell stories ... later."

Ms Percival pursed her lips, but Khia couldn't tell if she was displeased by McBride's story or was suppressing a smile.

"I was only trying to be friendly," he said. "Sheesh, guess I gotta watch everything I say in front of the kids, huh?" He smiled at Khia through the rear-view mirror, his blue eyes twinkling.

Khia reminded herself that she shouldn't let her guard down. She didn't know who she could trust. She wasn't even sure if she could trust Ms Percival. After all, they didn't really know her either; they had only met for the first time the previous week, when she'd picked them up in her silver and gold car—the one that was way too expensive for the salary of a social worker.

The tone of the conversation changed. While the adults were talking, Khia's attention narrowed onto her little brother. "And what do you think you were doing!" she whispered in his ear.

Devon shifted uncomfortably in his seat.

"Since when do we start holding strangers' hands and walking with them into cars?"

Devon turned red.

"Oh, don't be too hard on him," interjected the big man, named Norbert. "Truth is, I can be very persuasive ... especially when I have to be, and if he hadn't come willingly, I'd have picked him up screaming and squirming."

Khia watched as the man ruffled Devon's hair good-naturedly.

The young boy's laughter seemed to break the tension; even Ms Percival unpursed her lips and smiled.

Even though it was the last thing she felt like doing, Khia made herself smile, hoping it looked natural and not forced. On the inside Khia was baffled. She looked at the three adults, one at a time, trying to read them. Ms Percival, she guessed, was probably the hardest of the lot, and the least likely to allow Khia to get away with anything. The man driving the car was the softer of the two men, she surmised. She was sure that she wasn't sure of the big muscular man at all, except that Devon seemed to like him.

Ms Percival interrupted Khia's thoughts. "Allow me to formally introduce you to McBride," she motioned to the bald man at the wheel, "and Norbert." She nodded towards the big man sitting in the back seat with them.

Norbert offered his big hand to Khia in a handshake, and she felt her hand swallowed up by his. McBride followed Norbert's lead and shook their hands, all the while driving and keeping his eyes on the road.

"Believe me when I say this to you." Ms Percival slowed to add emphasis to her point, "I trust these two men with my life … and so can you."

Sure, thought Khia, sarcastically. *I'm supposed to believe that!*

"I apologize for our unusual tryst. Unfortunately, things have changed significantly. You are both in grave danger," she said in a somber voice.

Okay, that part she could believe … the danger part. She'd been sensing danger for quite some time now, especially in her dreams and considering all the strange things that had happened in the last seven days. But she didn't know if they were running *from* danger or *into* it.

"Ms Percival, what kind of danger are we in?" asked Khia pointedly.

"I can't explain it to you now," replied Ms Percival. "But you'll be safe with Norbert and McBride. They have been commissioned to take you to your grandmother's."

Grandmother!

Devon's face lit up, but the word reverberated through Khia's mind.

Up until that particular point in time, you see, Khia hadn't known they had a grandmother. Khia had always thought that she and her brother were all alone. *Could it be true?* No, Ms Percival had to be lying. There was no other explanation because … it just couldn't be true.

For a moment, Khia felt disorientated, like she was in a fairy tale … like *Little Red Riding Hood* … going into the dark dark forest to visit Grandma. Khia looked at the three adults in the car and another shiver of warning went through her. This was all wrong.

Breaking Khia's thoughts, Devon spoke excitedly, "Great! I've never had a grandmother before. What's she like? Is she real old? Does she make cookies? Will she tell us bedtime stories?" The questions poured out of him.

Abruptly, Norbert turned his head to watch the traffic flow by on the interstate, and there was a slight catch in Ms Percival's voice as she answered, "Yes … I've met your grandmother. She is very nice and you are very precious to her," Ms Percival reached over to touch Devon's cheek lightly with the tips of her well-manicured fingers. The gesture reminded Khia of a time when she'd had a family. On Sundays they'd go on family drives, with her father at the wheel, and her mother would turn around and check on them in the back seat, lovingly stroking their cheeks. Devon had been just a baby strapped in a car seat. That was before ... before the accident ...

"I haven't met a grand-mum yet that doesn't bake cookies," added McBride.

Norbert interrupted, "Let's not get too gushy. Can we conclude the formalities and get on with business, McBride," he barked "Let's get this show on the proverbial road."

Miles from nowhere, they were out of the car and seated at a roadside picnic area. It made Khia nervous how McBride kept checking around, as if he was expecting someone to show up, or something to happen, but there was no one else in the park except for a young man in a nearby field throwing a stick, that gyrated in a long arc, for his dog to fetch.

In the shade of a large oak tree, Khia shifted on the uncomfortable wooden park bench. She watched as Ms Percival opened her briefcase.

"These are their passports," she handed them to Norbert, along with an envelope. "This may come in handy."

Khia glanced at the passports and saw her black and white image displayed on the page—except Khia had never posed for the picture.

"Norbert will hold onto them," informed Ms Percival, "for safekeeping."

Ms Percival took off her designer shades and looked seriously at Khia. "I have already told you that you and your brother are no longer safe here," she emphasized. "The incident in the alley, and at the pond, were not accidents."

Amazement showed on Khia's face. *How does she know?*

"I'm sorry there is no time to explain."

As they quickly walked back to the car, Ms Percival handed McBride a thick envelope, "I trust you will spend this money wisely."

"Absolutely," answered McBride, unable to hide his smile.

Norbert shuffled uncomfortably, making Ms Percival laugh. Khia had never seen her laugh before, so it came as an odd but pleasant surprise.

At the car, Ms Percival knelt down and gave Devon a hug. Then Ms Percival went up to Khia and whispered, "Be smart, be careful, stay together, and trust Norbert and McBride. Do you understand, Khia?"

Khia nodded, but she was more confused than ever. She so wanted to believe Ms Percival.

"Until we meet again. Young knight, young lady," she took a step back and bowed.

"But Ms Percival," blurted out Khia. "What about the Brislings? What about our things? The church fire?"

"There's no time," answered Ms Percival. "You must go."

"But why didn't our grandmother come and get us herself?" asked Khia.

"Khia, I'm sorry," repeated Ms Percival, in a tone that invited no questions or arguments.

Khia's distrust resurfaced. *It's all rather too convenient*, she thought. *Don't ask any questions, just trust us. This is crap*, thought Khia angrily; she didn't buy it for one second.

McBride got into the car and revved the engine, "Khia, you want to sit in the front?"

Like a real gentleman, Norbert held the door open for her. Khia would have rather been in the back with Devon but quietly sat in the front seat.

Devon waved shyly to Ms Percival and took the big man's hand. They got into the back seat of the car and Khia heard Norbert say, "Right kid, you're now officially eight, so no car seat for you, okay?"

"Okay," Devon repeated happily. He liked being a year older, he felt grown up.

Khia thought about everything that had happened, and how quickly her brother had taken to Norbert. Devon was so young and innocent; Khia huffed to herself with annoyance. How on earth was she going to protect him now? She saw her small sour face reflected in the car's side window.

Ms Percival stood alone, her arm raised in farewell, and shouted urgently to them, "God speed!"

CHAPTER 7

Road Trip

Take a train, take a plane, walk, hike,
watch the world go by.
All the time wishing you were home but itching to go,
some... place,
any... place,
any place but here.
Out here on the road...
watching worlds go by.

It was a less than auspicious start. In fact, they had hardly left the parking lot when Devon announced, "I got to go pee." Then added, "Real bad!"

McBride laughed out loud.

Norbert gave Devon a stern and disbelieving look. "You have got to be kidding. You had all the time in the world when we were in the park. Why didn't you go then, when you had the chance?"

Devon's lower lip quivered.

Norbert softened his tone but still sounded thunderous and overbearing. "How badly do you really have to go? Can you hold it a little longer ... say an hour?"

"You negotiating with the kid?" said an amused McBride, looking at the two of them in his rear-view mirror.

Squirming in the back seat left no doubt as to the urgency. Khia turned around in her seat, ready to say something to Norbert, when McBride interjected, "Come on Norbert, he's just a kid. Don't you remember what it was like?" He chuckled.

"No, actually I don't," responded Norbert curtly.

Devon gave Norbert an innocent smile, along with his sad puppy dog eyes.

No match for the seven year old, Norbert conceded, "McBride, pull over. It appears we have an emergency that requires immediate attention."

"No kidding," muttered McBride, who had already slowed the car and was pulling over onto the gravel shoulder.

Khia looked around. This could be her chance.

Norbert shook his head. "Why did I agree to this job? Kids."

McBride laughed out loud.

"You finding this funny," said Norbert.

"Yeah."

He has a nice infectious laugh, thought Khia.

The car door opened and Devon shot out behind a tree.

This was her chance … but before she could even unclip her seatbelt and open the door, Norbert (as if he had read her mind) put his large hand on her shoulder and said, "I wouldn't do that if I were you."

Moments later, Devon streaked back into the waiting car. While he fumbled with the seatbelt buckle, McBride waited patiently, as if they had all of the time in the world.

"Seatbelts on!" shouted McBride. "Yes! Road trip!" They zoomed off in a shower of loose stones and dust.

Khia thought that McBride seemed like a really nice man. He had a playful sense of humor and it was hard not to like him. He had this mischievous smile, so you were never quite sure what he was going to do next. He was of average height and had a sturdy frame, but Norbert was entirely different. He was big and intimidating; he had to be about six foot four, with broad muscular shoulders, and he had a large wicked scar down the left side of his cheek that added to his ferocious appearance. She knew she wouldn't want to get on his wrong side, but Devon seemed to have formed an attachment to him. She couldn't figure that one out. *Norbert? Why would Devon pick Norbert? Wouldn't McBride have been the better choice?*

"How about we stop at the next town to pick up food and supplies for the road trip?" suggested McBride.

Norbert nodded in agreement and pulled out a map.

"Can I see?" asked Devon.

"Sure," Norbert said, opening the map. There was hardly any room in the back seat, with Norbert, the map, and Devon peering over. Norbert showed Devon where they were and where they were going. "What's the name of this place?" he pointed.

"D-dic-," stuttered Devon, as he stumbled over the word. Getting all red in the face, he turned away and muttered, "I can't read."

"Ah, it's okay kid, you're seven, uh, I mean eight," said McBride, which made Devon smile.

"Too many syllables in Dickinson anyway," said Norbert.

"It took him longer to read you know," said McBride about Norbert, "and now he's considered somewhat of an expert. He'll teach you. No worries!"

"No worries?" Norbert whispered in Devon's ear, "I think he got that line from some movie."

Devon laughed.

"By the time we get to your grandmother's house, you'll be reading like a pro," said McBride. "Norbert and I will make sure of it. It's why we're so loved everywhere we go. We fulfill our contracts above and beyond what's called for."

"Or needed," added Norbert.

"So ... ah ... where're we going?" interrupted Khia.

"We're going to your grandmother's. I thought we made that clear," replied Norbert.

"No," said Khia, a little annoyed. "Where does she live?"

"We're going to the center of the world," said McBride, "the Big Enchilada, the city that never sleeps, the Big Apple."

"New York City," Norbert and McBride said in unison.

"Jinx," said McBride.

And Devon laughed.

So why do we need passports? thought Khia.

McBride continued, "Although, I wonder sometimes how long it will remain the center of the world. I gather you've never been to Beijing or Shanghai. Interesting cities and fast-rising stars. It won't be too long before another one becomes the center of this world. So many beautiful cities ... London, Paris, Constantinople ..."

"It's Istanbul now," corrected Norbert.

"Ah right, Istanbul," McBride looked at him in the rear-view mirror, "and there was Rome, Babylon, Alexandria, Ur, they all had their day. New York today ... Beijing tomorrow. Who knows?"

"Is this a history lesson or a road trip?" quipped Norbert.

"Is New York where our grandmother lives?" Khia persisted.

"No," they both answered at the same time.

"Jinx," cried out McBride.

Devon howled with laughter.

Letting her guard down, just a little, Khia couldn't help but smile. Maybe Devon knew something she didn't know. It was hard not to like (and trust) these two very unusual characters.

†

In the town of Dickinson, Norbert took the kids to a local diner, where they had the greasy special: burgers and fries. McBride passed on the trans-fat and went off on his own to trade in their black sedan for a vehicle that had a little more power.

In less than an hour, McBride returned with a new, dark blue, two-tone Chevy V8, 4-wheel drive truck with extended cab, over-sized tires, stainless steel step-plates, and a matching colored wedge cap.

"Uh McBride," said Norbert, who looked on in disbelief at McBride's choice in vehicle. "I thought you said we needed a vehicle that was inconspicuous."

"No, I said more power."

"How much did this put us back?" asked Norbert.

"Ms P. gave us a Platinum Card," said McBride. "That beautiful, foolish, and intelligent woman," he added, smiling broadly.

"You promised Ms Percival you'd use the money wisely," chastised Norbert. "McBride, give me the card," he said, snatching the card out of McBride's hand. "And the cash ... hand over the cash. NOW!" he bellowed.

Reluctantly, McBride pulled out a wad of cash, but a second later he skipped out of reach, flashing a second credit card—a gold card that he had every intention of keeping.

"McBride, you have half an hour to finish your shopping," said Norbert.

"Half an hour! The expert shopper that I am, that gives me plenty of time," replied McBride.

A roguish smile played on Norbert's face. It was a look that Khia had, until that point, only seen on McBride.

Norbert, spotting Rita's Fine Clothes and Outfitters, said to Khia and Devon, "We're going ... there."

†

In precisely half an hour, Norbert, Khia, and Devon emerged from Rita's Fine Clothes and Outfitters, looking a wondrous sight, dressed in new and stylish clothes, wearing designer shades, and carrying a number of shopping bags. Norbert wore a well-cut Italian suit, and Devon was the pint-size mirror image right down to his leather shoes. Khia had discarded her grayish-white dress for a pure white dress and shiny new shoes. The only thing missing was the music as they strutted towards McBride, who was waiting for them by the truck.

They'd look spiffy for New York City when they saw their grandmother. However, it should be noted that, in their shopping bags, Norbert had also purchased more practical things like jeans, shirts, coats, and hiking boots ... just in case.

In the meantime, McBride had gone to the local hardware store for supplies, after he'd gone to the grocery store for food and water, and true to his word about being a good shopper, had even managed to pick up a few books for the kids.

"What you get me?" asked McBride.

Norbert tossed McBride a baseball cap and cheap plastic pink shades.

"Where's my suit?" asked McBride.

"They didn't have your size," retorted Norbert.

"But they had yours!" replied McBride.

†

Stopping and shopping in Dickinson turned out to be both a good thing and a bad thing. It helped the local economy of the slowly dying town, as the car dealership, the local hardware store, and Rita's Fine Clothes and Outfitters all benefited. But they had made an impression that would be long remembered.

It would only take a few hours for someone who was persistent, clever, and well connected to put it all together: information extrapolated from Rita's Fine Clothes and Outfitters; the car dealership; and an amiable conversation with the local gas station attendant, Warren T. Smith, a genial old man who made it a point to know everyone's business. After all, it wasn't every day that an odd quartet arrived in one vehicle and left in another: a blue two-tone Chevy truck with over-sized wheels.

Norbert and McBride knew they were leaving a paper trail in Dickinson. They believed what had been gained in speed and surprise would be worth the risk. However, if they had known who was following, they would have been a bit more careful ... but then again, maybe not, since that wasn't exactly their style.

As they left the small town, Khia once again noticed how often McBride checked his rear-view mirror. It made her feel nervous, and she remembered Ms Percival's words: *Be smart, be careful, stay together, and trust Norbert and McBride.*

After miles on the road, they settled into a lull, soothed by the back and forth motion of the truck as it sped along the highway, the blur of yellow and white lines on the asphalt, and the signs that marked their journey.

†

That night, they stopped in a small motel. Stretching their legs, the kids ran about like maniacs. Around eleven, well past Devon's bedtime, things finally grew quiet and Norbert read the young boy a bedtime story. Khia, lying with her eyes closed in the other single bed, listened. Soon both kids drifted off to sleep, or so he thought.

Norbert turned off the lights and left their room, leaving the adjoining door slightly ajar. *It might not be such a tough assignment after all,* he thought.

"What sweet kids," commented Norbert.

"You're just saying that because they're sleeping. I thought you didn't like kids," laughed McBride.

"I don't," replied Norbert gruffly.

"Yeah, that's what I thought."

"Do you think we lost them?" Norbert asked, parting the vinyl blinds to take a look outside.

"Not likely, but who knows?" shrugged McBride.

"It'll take us at least three days to get to New York," assessed Norbert, "taking the secondary roads and keeping to the speed limit."

"Maybe we should have flown, or driven straight through and not stopped," offered McBride.

"No. Flying's too dangerous, too many check points," said Norbert. "As we get closer, the risks will become greater. Odds are always against us, but we manage, eh McBride?"

"Have you thought more about taking a detour?" asked McBride. "We could go to Nora's."

"We'll head north and parallel the border. If there's trouble, we'll cross the border and drop Nora a visit."

"Sounds like a plan. I'll take the first watch," offered McBride.

†

At about three o'clock in the morning, no one heard soft footsteps crossing the room. A hand closed tightly over Devon's mouth. Devon opened his eyes wide, unable to scream.

CHAPTER 8

Something Evil Rises

...centuries of stony sleep
Were vexed to nightmare by a rocking cradle,
And what rough beast, its hour come round at last,
The Second Coming, William Butler Yeats, 1919

At about the same time that Norbert was reading Devon a bedtime story, unusual activities were taking place in the ruins of a burnt-out church. Two figures, silhouetted by the rising moon, passed undetected under yellow crime-scene tape.

†

The Fire Department had had a very difficult time containing the blaze. It had taken the coordinated efforts of four fire halls systematically attacking the fire from many angles to check its advance. The church conflagration had raged for hours. Aired on the local and national evening news were images of the burning church ... tornadoes of flames, billowing smoke, and sparks of fireworks. By the time the flames had subsided, the inside of the church had been completely gutted.

As with all suspicious fires, the chief Fire Marshall of the region was called.

On Sundays, the Fire Marshall typically spent the day with his family. However, Fire Marshall Ladkey was a man dedicated to his work; he took the call in the middle of his meal. It wasn't long before he put on his fire chief's hat, said goodbye to his wife and kids, and went to the site.

For a long time, the Fire Marshall stood in the blackened church basement.

The late afternoon sunlight penetrated the area like swords of light. Parts of the ceiling had collapsed, leaving a large hole where a slow steady stream of water and mist spilled into the basement and slithered towards a dark pool.

Fire Marshall Ladkey had been a fireman for over twenty years. There had never been a fire that he could not explain, but this particular fire puzzled him. At first, he tried to slough it off, dismiss the feeling as being due to the sacredness of the place, yet he knew this wasn't quite true; it was something more—something he could feel but couldn't explain. Ladkey knew that all fires had a story to tell, sometimes revealed hidden buried things, and sometimes revealed things that were better left forgotten.

A cursory investigation had revealed nothing that could logically explain the fire's origins. In fact, all indications told him that it had started in the very foundation of the church itself. But that, he knew, was impossible. Fire needed a spark, electrical wires, gas pipes, heat, or combustibles to start, to grow, and to sustain its life, but all the signs nevertheless pointed to rock and stone—rock and stone that had been laid over a hundred years before.

Glass crunched under his feet; despite the destruction, he found the scene strangely beautiful. The fact that there was so much glass also contradicted the Fire Marshall's suspicions. At first, he had thought the glass was from the blown-out stain glass windows, but upon further investigation he was convinced that the multicolored glass was indeed created by the fire. This would be consistent with the extreme high temperature ... but that was impossible. In non-industrial fires, with few solvents and volatile chemicals, only small amounts of glass could possibly be created.

Ladkey crouched a few feet away from the edge of the murky pool of water. His considerable knowledge and instincts told him that this was where the fire had started. Yet it didn't feel right; his instincts also told him not to go any closer. Ladkey taught younger firefighters about fires. His mantra was to respect fire—respect it for what it could do, for its power and its mystery, and for its ability to kill men, women, children, and most especially ... firefighters. The Fire Marshall had seen it too often. And Fire Marshall Ladkey understood fire better than most, and so he knew when to leave things well enough alone, to wait, and to let the embers cool and die.

†

Unknown to the Fire Marshall, a small creature—a rare kind of Sylph, a creature of primordial fire—was tucked inside a small hard glass egg below the waterline of the murky pool, and it looked out at him from its small kaleidoscopic window.

Silently it watched through its fuzzy colored shell as the Fire Marshall approached. It heard its own long dormant heartbeat quicken for the first time. It had been brought to life by the searing flame; the intense heat had incubated it from its long, long sleep. Yet the heat that should have brought it forth had been extinguished too soon. It was weak and frightened.

When the Fire Marshall abruptly left, it was a relief to it, and it curled itself more comfortably in its shell, wrapping its tail more tightly about its small shivering body trying to conserve the fading warmth.

It waited.

Not turning his back, the Fire Marshall retreated from the murky pool. He wasn't sure why he was suddenly in such a foul mood, stomping away from the church. "Absolutely no one, NO ONE, goes into this church until I return," he barked out angry orders to his firefighters and police officials. "Tape up the area."

His intent was to return the next morning with a crew to complete the investigation, but it never happened. Strangely, the day was filled with priorities needing his immediate attention, so it wasn't until later the following day that he managed to assemble a team to complete his investigation.

†

Two figures with powerful flashlights walked through the skeletal remains of the burnt-out church. With purpose, they made their way into the basement, crunching over debris to the very spot where the Fire Marshall had stood many hours before. From one flashlight, a silver light (like a halo) illuminated the murky pool, while the other panned the room like a spotlight on a theater stage, illuminating the multicolored fragments of glass. Eventually both beams of light settled on the oily water of the pool. Without haste, but with due caution, one of them dipped a sturdy metal rod into the opaque water. The rod clipped something that sounded like a hollow bell. A couple of sharp stabs with the metal rod and the shell casing cracked.

There was a small high-pitched popping sound, and then the frightened creature exploded from its hard glass shell, intent on killing the thing that had disturbed it. It burst out from the water like a hungry Poseidon missile.

But the woman had anticipated such an action and expertly caught the creature, by the scruff of its thin neck, in mid-flight. It would have taken little effort to snap its neck … and end its existence. The Sylph whimpered and cried pathetically; its tail flailed about trying to inflict harm. Weak and winded, it coiled itself around the woman's arm and squeezed.

"Well Katrina, what do you think," spoke Ezrulie. "Beautiful aren't they? And so rare in this part of the world."

The young girl was enthralled by such a magnificent red and gold creature. She reached out her hand and felt its dry hot skin. The creature was no more than eighteen inches long from its head to the very tip of its tail. "Oh it's so beautiful," Katrina cooed, her eyes aglow. "How ever did it get here?"

"Most church foundations have any number of such creatures hidden in their foundations, but few are ever called into existence. This one has been here only a little while … a hundred and fifty or two hundred years, no more. There are magnificent specimens still to be found in the foundations and catacombs of the great churches of Europe—in fact, all around the world, especially in the great holy places like Vatican City, Jerusalem, Constantinople, Moscow, Medina. They can be dangerous, and difficult to control, but this little one is nothing. Rather weak right now, but it's feisty." The Sylph struggled and whimpered helplessly.

Ezrulie's iron grip held it securely. "Hmmmm," she appraised it, "I should think it will serve our purpose."

"Are you ready, my dear?" Ezrulie paused. "This creature must bond with you now," she said, in a voice that sounded almost maternal but underneath contained overtones of cold cruelty that were deeply embedded, "otherwise, it will not survive."

Katrina nodded and did something that seemed, at first, very strange. She slowly unbuttoned the first few buttons of her dress. Ezrulie brought the Sylph near. With a sharp claw the creature slashed Katrina.

The young girl's blood flowed freely. It clamped onto Katrina and began sucking her rich red blood. Satisfying its great hunger, the Sylph calmed.

The young girl cradled the creature as if it were her baby that was slurping, sucking, hiccuping, and burping. The Sylph looked into Katrina's eyes, seeing its protector for the first time—the one who gave it life.

In that moment, the creature bonded with Katrina. It was a bond not easily broken. This creature would do anything for the one it loved. Anything.

"Come Katrina, we must go."

Ezrulie, and Katrina cradling the Sylph, walked undetected from the ruins of the church into the nearby cemetery. Amongst the cold tombstones, the Sylph continued to feed greedily. It lasted for about twenty more minutes until, at last satiated, the Sylph stopped its feeding and released the young girl from its grip.

If there had been a little more light, one would have seen that Katrina was getting paler and paler from the loss of the fluids that were sucked so readily from her. For a few moments, she wondered if she would survive this feeding frenzy, from this unholy child, but as Ezrulie had informed her, it would never need such an offering again. Sylphs quickly learned to fend for themselves.

Katrina placed the little creature on the ground and staunched the flow of blood from her wound. She felt a little unsteady and sat weakly with her back resting on a tombstone, where earlier that day Norbert had rested his hand talking to Devon. The coldness of the tombstone helped Katrina to maintain her consciousness. In a dreamlike state, she had an image of a powerful angel come to deliver her to the doors of heaven. She forced herself to focus her attention on Ezrulie, who brought out a small clear plastic bag from her pocket and handed it to her.

Katrina, with trembling hands, broke the seal.

Staying very close to Katrina, the creature calmly swished its tail back and forth. Katrina brought Devon's baseball cap to its sensitive nose. The Sylph breathed in the aromas that were locked inside. Deeply it breathed in the thousands of different fragrances and the many human hands that had touched this piece of cloth. Aromas of a small boy, an Australian shepherd, a little girl, and fainter smells that were farther away: of a retail sales clerk, a seamstress, workers in warehouses and ports around the world, and even the aroma of a young child who had picked the cotton and a peasant farmer who had planted the seed. All these pictures sprang into the mind of the Sylph, but the most overpowering smell of all, the sweetest scent, was of a little boy.

"Seek," said Katrina, in a surprisingly strong and cruel voice. "Seek ..." Katrina looked at Ezrulie.

"And kill," said Ezrulie.

"He's just a little boy," said Katrina.

"And kill," repeated Ezrulie.

Katrina paused.

"Say it," said Ezrulie.

"And kill," said Katrina to the Sylph.

The Sylph, before their very eyes, began to change into the images of the people who had touched the cloth and had left their signature. The creature searched and separated the wheat from the chaff, the insignificant and the important. Again, it breathed in the scents that lingered on the cap.

Before their eyes, the Sylph transformed into a boy who was remarkably close in size and appearance to Devon, who was (at that moment) soundly sleeping hundreds of miles away, after having been read a bedtime story.

The Devon-like creature stood before Katrina, and smiled and laughed just like Devon, but if one looked closely at this shape-shifter, the strange evil glint in its eyes could not be masked.

"Good," said Ezrulie, sounding quite satisfied.

Katrina looked deeply into the eyes of this, her most unnatural child, and lovingly caressed its hot cheek. She brought the creature closer to her, kissing it before she whispered into its ear, "Seek and kill. For your Mommy ... for your Mommy," and she giggled, glancing at Ezrulie.

The Sylph knew what Katrina wanted and it laughed, copying its mother's laugh, and then smiled, very much like Devon would have smiled.

†

Onlookers would have been quite intrigued by the actions of this young boy in the cemetery that night, because in some ways the boy acted like a dog sniffing the wind and the ground, searching for a scent in a world of caustic industrial chemicals and solvents among the sweet natural smells of trees and plants and the skeletal remains of the dead. Chaotically, or so it seemed, it ran around the graveyard; then it abruptly stopped. Remarkably, it had found something ... not much, just a whiff in the breeze, and with haunting intensity, it focused its eyes and (with a wild cry) set off in pursuit of its prey.

Katrina turned to Ezrulie, "It's going the wrong way. It's going towards the White Hills."

"Patience my dear," Ezrulie answered. "It knows what to do."

"It's so little," commented Katrina, sounding like a new mother separated from her baby for the first time.

"It will grow quickly," the older woman responded.

In the distance, they heard the angry growls of a dog, followed by a sudden loud yelp.

"What was that?" asked Katrina.

"It has to eat," smiled Ezrulie. "Transformation requires energy."

Accepting the answer, Katrina followed Ezrulie and stepped silently into the waiting black car.

†

In the underground parking lot of Ezrulie's penthouse apartment, a car pulled up.

"Lady Ezrulie," Mr. Elliot got out of the car, "your report." He handed her two red folders. The folders contained information gleaned by Blackwood Corporation. Information about Khia and Devon Ashworth: dates of birth, addresses, phone numbers, and all manner of pertinent and ancillary information that also included information on a certain social worker—a Ms Percival.

"Yes, Ms Percival," spoke Ezrulie, looking over the files. "Gentlemen," she looked at Cocklebur and Burdock, "I trust you will be paying her a visit."

"But of course," Cocklebur answered menacingly.

Ezrulie looked at Cocklebur. "The young lady requires some medical assistance. See to it."

Cocklebur opened a small metal case. He motioned to Katrina, who was barely conscious, having lost a lot of blood, and pushed her against the car.

"Drink this," said Burdock. "It's sweet."

Ezrulie turned to the pale thin man. "Mr. Elliot, I understand your corporate masters have profited well since our last collaboration. Subcontracting military equipment is lucrative and the mercenary business is booming these days, is it not?"

"It is a complex world we live in," Mr. Elliot said noncommittally. "We are humble servants and Blackwood simply provides a service. Ultimately, we serve a higher purpose. May I remind you, Lady Ezrulie, that our executives are religious men ... men of conviction who take their responsibilities ... seriously."

"Yes, yes, I know," said Ezrulie dismissing his rhetoric. "Remind me again Mr. Elliot," she asked folding her arms, "what is it that you can do for me?"

"Globally, we have access to governments, corporations, and media, as well as national security databases, communication networks, situation rooms, to name just a few. For a reasonable fee, a single phone call can set things in motion. I propose we use the media."

"Continue," said Ezrulie.

"By this time tomorrow, images and names of the two children will be splashed across television screens and front pages of newspapers across the country. 'Abducted by pedophiles' should get the right reaction. In such a groundswell of public and national sentiment, our truant children and those who protect them will find it rather difficult to escape the net that has been cast."

Ezrulie smiled wickedly. She was pleased.

"Blackwood has tens of thousands of men and women in its employ, many in high positions of power. They are paid to follow orders, not to ask questions. Lady Ezrulie, it shall be quite a miracle if they make it to New York City."

"Then it appears we have a business arrangement, Mr. Elliot."

Cocklebur tossed away the stainless-steel half-circle suturing needle, stained with a drop of red. It pinged off the ground, coming to rest between them.

He looked at his handiwork. It would leave a scar. He didn't care.

Ezrulie turned to Katrina and said demandingly, "Come."

Katrina, her wound throbbing, followed Ezrulie to the elevator, clinging limply to her favorite doll.

CHAPTER 9

Lady's Knight

Often, in the too many foster homes Khia and Devon had lived in, they had practiced stealth. Khia had taught Devon to lie still and feign sleep, and taught him how to move without making a sound, but no matter how hard she tried, she hadn't been able to teach him how to keep his mouth shut. He could stay calm in all sorts of sticky situations, and they had achieved a level of sneaky success that many people would have been surprised by, and others appalled at. For someone like Norbert, this quality would have been greatly admired ... if he hadn't been the one who had been duped.

Earlier that evening, you may recall that Khia and Devon had run amok in the motel room, jumping on beds, and opening and slamming doors and drawers. Khia had been testing more than her guardians' patience; she had also been testing her surroundings for sounds like squeaks, bumps, and thumps.

Norbert and McBride, it is reasonable to say, had been taken aback by their energetic play, but then again, they hadn't had a lot of experience with kids. It was a mystery to them why kids did the things they did.

Devon was, however, familiar with his sister's tactics. The giveaway was the pattern: how often Khia rolled off her bed, moved towards his bed, and then to the door. Mixing it up, Khia ran in great circles through the room, encouraging her brother to do the same, all the while laughing and screaming in apparent natural wonder and delight.

Devon wanted to tell Norbert, but one look from his sister and he remained silent.

So when Khia clamped her hand over his mouth in the middle of the night, he hadn't been really scared.

Guided by a thin beam of light, shining through the door between the adjoining rooms, Devon and his sister tiptoed across the floor.

Nothing stirred.

†

Slumped uncomfortably in a chair, Norbert shook his head, trying to shake off his sleepiness. He didn't need a lot of sleep, but he and McBride had traveled a great distance and had been going almost full out for awhile.

Stretching his back, Norbert got up to check the darkened room; he didn't question the outline of two still and sleeping forms. Safe, sound, and secure under their blankets. *Poor little mites*, he foolishly thought, *they must be exhausted.*

He went to the window, and parted the blinds. All was quiet except for the soft hum of the air-conditioner. He did not see the two figures that pressed themselves against the wall.

It wasn't until later that Norbert's mind put the pieces together. Too still. Too quiet. No hands. People don't sleep without at least one hand poking outside of the blankets, even in the coldest weather.

"Oh for the love of God." He'd been tricked by an adolescent. "McBride! Wake up!" he called from the other room, as he yanked off the covers from the two beds—the white sheets flowing in the air like the wings of an angel. "We have a world-class emergency on our hands. The rotten little cons have escaped." He paced across the room. "And I let them walk right by me. If we don't do something quick, they could be dead within the hour."

"Wow! They're good," McBride, awake and alert, gathered his things. "Slipped right through you, huh?" he chuckled.

"Not the right time, McBride," a dangerous glaring look from Norbert put an end to any misplaced, yet potentially humorous, comments.

McBride cleared his throat, choking back his words, "Right then, I'll get the truck."

"I'll track them on foot," answered Norbert. "They can't be far. I'll meet you on the street."

Norbert stormed out of the room and looked down on the empty parking lot. He didn't see the kids, but he didn't see anything out of the ordinary either; that was good. It meant they weren't in danger ... yet! He flew down the stairs, four at a time, looking for any signs that Khia and Devon left behind.

"That's it. Straight to New York, no detours, no stopping," Norbert grumbled under his breath. "I'll put them in chains if I have to."

Norbert went around the building, looking for clues. Khia and Devon may have perfected the art of escape, but they were careless on the run.

The night was cool and moisture from the still night had condensed onto the grass. It wasn't long before he saw a small footprint, where a small shoe had briefly strayed off the sidewalk and touched the grass. "Jeez," he thought, "when I get my hands on them, I'll have to teach them a thing or two."

As Norbert pursued his charges, he saw more clues that told him he was closing in: a squished bug, another that was squashed, and an overturned dry stone. Small signs, that few would have noticed, were like large billboards to Norbert—signs that pointed him in the right direction.

†

She'd been known by many names throughout her professional life, but the name that she'd earned on the street—the name that had in essence chosen her—was Catherine the Great.

Like Khia, Catherine had been in foster care, taken away from her mother and the only home she had ever known.

From a very early age, Catherine had come to accept her life, and had given up trying to justify, or understand, her dysfunctional childhood and her troubled mother.

Catherine's mother had been a drug addict and had become a prostitute to enable her habit or perhaps it had been the other way around. As far back as Catherine could remember, she'd been placed in front of the television set while her mother went out at night. Catherine, clinging to a dirty terrycloth towel, would cuddle up to the television set and fall asleep.

Her mother would return, sometimes with bruises on her body, and some-times with bruises on her face—injuries that sometimes took a few days, a few weeks, or even a lifetime to heal.

What was hardest to forgive and forget was not the neglect or the abuse, but those rare moments when her mother would hold her tightly in her arms to tell her how much she loved her. Lies. Her mother had needed the comfort, and Catherine would find herself saying, "Don't cry Mommy. Don't cry. Everything's going to be all right … everything's going to be all right."

So when the authorities took her mother away, Catherine remembered it like it was yesterday. Torn. It was supposed to be for the better, they said, and that everything would be all right. Empty words. Lies.

Silently, she had held onto the social worker's hand, separated from her terrycloth towel. Hiding the hurt, and the turmoil within her, and never able to shut out her mother's murderous screams; they followed her in nightmares for years to come. And then one day she was told that her mother had died. Few details were given, in the belief that Catherine was far too young to understand.

By the time Catherine was Khia's age, she'd gone from foster home to foster home and had run away so often that eventually she had no place left to run. That's when she realized that it was impossible to escape yourself and she stopped running. Catherine also learned that she was stronger and smarter than her mother. She didn't need the drugs—which provided the temporary euphoria of forgetting—that her mother had so desperately needed. Catherine wanted to remember; Catherine needed to remember.

†

Nearing thirty, Catherine had spent nearly half her life on the street that the locals called the Storefront—euphemistically named because of all the "candy" and product that was on display. Catherine had acquired the Storefront the old fashioned way: by wresting it from others. It had been difficult, especially at the beginning. There had been frequent confronta-tions, but they had underestimated her, and assumed that was too young, too weak, and too innocent.

By her natural intelligence, calculated friendships, strategic coalitions, and (make no mistake about it) the necessary use of money and violence, Catherine had been able to enact the unwritten laws of the street and thus had secured her rights. And, in so doing, she achieved a degree of protection and respect for herself and the tough-shelled but vulnerable young women who also called the streets their home. Amongst the women of the trade, she was known as a generous woman, and had helped many young women get off the street. They were known as either "The Chosen" or "Catherine's Chosen" and they were the ones who were able to leave that world behind.

†

The night had been quiet, which was all the more reason to stay vigilant. Sitting on concrete steps, Catherine was with her friend Shady, who was (informally) her second-in-command. Shady, chewing gum because she had quit smoking, was about to call it a night.

Catherine wore a short red dress that seemed painted on and wore her thick blond hair down around her shoulders. All of it was a fantasy of crafted clothes, hair, makeup, props, and accessories: tricks of the trade.

Shady had just stood to leave when they saw something they didn't expect to see at 3:30 in the morning, especially in this part of town: two kids walking quickly, with the young boy running every couple of steps to keep up with the girl.

†

Once Khia and her brother had escaped from the motel room, the flaw in her plan had become apparent: she didn't know what to do, or where to go. And what was worse was that she wasn't even sure where they were!

Leaving the motel grounds, they reached a sidewalk. Grabbing her brother's hand, Khia arbitrarily chose a direction and they started walking. Ten minutes later, they wandered onto a well-lit street that was lined on both sides with various hotels, and their multi-colored flashing lights. This is where they saw Shady, with her dark hair in a bouffant style and her fashionable floral dress, and Catherine, with her big hair, big breasts, and tiny teeny tight red dress.

In an extremely exaggerated southern accent, Shady was the one who greeted them, "Well aren't you the pair. Don't you two know this ain't the road to Kansas?"

Shady was like a character out of a book, but which character? There were so many parts to her personality. Like all of us, she had some good and bad qualities. When she was good she was real good, and when she was bad, well … she was real bad, but there were some who would say that when she was bad she was 'better'. Shady was no coward and could be as fierce as a lioness if the need arose—and believe you me, she'd arisen to this fierceness on a few occasions. Most of all, however, Shady was smart, and had a really big heart, although few people ever knew it. No one, you see, really knew Shady (the real person inside) except, perhaps, for Catherine. And the loyalty that Shady had for Catherine … well she would go to the ends of the world for her, and do anything … all Catherine had to do was ask.

"Hello, I'm Shady and this is Catherine the Great. Now if you've got a problem, she's the one who can solve it, or at least point you in the right direction." Shady patted the step, "So why don't you sit down here beside us and tell us your problem. We're very good listeners," she said encouragingly.

Having been in a few too many discerning church-going, middle-class, foster-home families, Khia knew who such women were, and she knew that the best course of action would be to keep on walking. Unfortunately, Devon didn't know this and stopped.

"Why would you think we have a problem?" asked Khia.

"Why would a young lady in waiting, with her young page, be wandering the streets so late at night," said Catherine, in a gentle voice, "if not for a problem." She smiled at Devon.

"Hello," said Devon, letting go of Khia's hand. "I'm Devon and this is my sister Khia," he said. "We're running away."

"Is that so," responded Catherine.

"It's my sister's idea. We're going to visit our grandmother. She lives in a really big apple." He was about to blurt out more when he caught his sister's glare. Devon clamped his mouth shut, but it was too late.

Oh, what was the use? thought Khia, and sat down on the stairs between Catherine and Shady.

The story came out in a mishmash, as Khia and Devon spilled over their words and interrupted each other, trying to explain what had happened, adding important and not-so-important details. They told Catherine and Shady everything: that they were foster kids; about their recent mishaps and adventures, including what had happened in the alley with the bag lady; going to the creepy pond with Snowden; Father Tobias and the fire at the church; as well as Ms Percival, their new social worker, and the two men who were taking them to New York City to see their grandmother ... but that they didn't have a grandmother so she couldn't actually live in New York City.

Catherine and Shady may have been confused by the story, so quickly and so badly told, but the two of them knew that the kids were in some kind of trouble and that was enough. So, by the time Norbert jogged into view and entered the fray, intending to take full control of the situation, all hell was on the verge of breaking loose.

"Whoa, back off," yelled Shady, no longer sounding like a southern belle.

Catherine confronted the large muscular man. "And who are you," she said sarcastically, standing between him and the kids, "their uncle?"

"The name's Norbert," he answered, in as polite a voice as he could muster, which wasn't very polite at all. Norbert tried to smile as he assessed the situation; he could tell the two kids had somehow managed, in an incredibly short time, to get these ladies of the night to become both allies and advocates. *Not bad, not bad at all,* he thought. He had learned two things that night: One, he had woefully underestimated Khia, and two, in this situation he required a particular kind of finesse, and for that he would need McBride.

Devon was happy to see Norbert, but Khia was rather alarmed at how quickly he had found them.

"Listen you!" Catherine moved aggressively close to him, poking her finger into his chest. If the situation hadn't been so serious, it would have looked rather comical—her small stature next to his big bulk—but she wasn't fazed at all.

Norbert took a step back.

"I'm telling you how it's going to go," said Catherine. "I'm going to call the police and they will settle this whole matter. Do you understand?"

Norbert towered over her, "Good," he said, trying his best to act indifferent, but he wasn't very good at that. "Call the police." But getting the police involved was the worst thing possible. *Where is McBride?* Norbert weighed the options. He could easily knock out the two ladies of the night, grab the two kids, and make a run for it, but he had a much bigger problem. What would it take to get Khia to trust him?

Fortunately, for Norbert, at that very moment, a big Chevy truck (driving on the wrong side of the street) arrived with a loud squeal of tires, completing a perfect one hundred and eighty degree turn, and creating lots of smoke that filled the place with the acrid smell of burnt rubber. The grand entrance stopped their angry words, leaving them all staring with gaping mouths.

Shady, back to her southern belle accent, shouted to the driver, "The Storefront's closed Mister! Now git your sweet ass out of here and come back tomorrow!"

The truck window slowly rolled down and a man with a bald head leaned out. He was smiling with a grin that ran from one end of his face to the other. He called out, "Hey! Norbert, hear that? I have a sweet ass."

"McBride, cut the theatrics; we're kind of busy here," bawled Norbert.

"Hello, Catherine. How about some sympathy for my friend," McBride motioned to Norbert.

"Well I'll be," said Catherine, who sashayed over to the truck. She leaned in and gave the bald man a big kiss on the lips. Breathlessly, she asked, "And what brings you to my doorstep, Mickey McB?"

"Why, beautiful," he answered, "I've lost two little ones," he paused, "three, if you count the big one."

"Are you going to tell me what this is all about?" asked Catherine.

With a twinkle in his blue eyes, he said, "Ladies, do you want to join us … for breakfast that is." He winked. "There must be a place that's serving at this time of the morning."

†

All of them piled into the two-toned blue truck. And so the evening of the great escape, which Khia had premeditated, hadn't turned out the way she had expected.

After dropping Shady off, Catherine directed them to a diner that was open 24/7. Catherine disappeared into the restroom and emerged a few minutes later transformed. She had removed her makeup, tied up her hair in a ponytail, and wore jeans and a T-shirt. Where she got the jeans and T-shirt no one was quite sure.

Catherine sat next to McBride and held his hand, "I've missed you," she said, and the conversation began in earnest.

Khia listened quietly, while Norbert gently laid the very tired Devon on an adjacent vinyl booth and covered him with his black leather coat.

Khia noted how McBride treated Catherine with respect, not passing judgment as she had done earlier. She also discovered that she really liked Catherine, and came to understand, at least a little that night, why Catherine's friends called her "the Great".

"I've read the papers. The entire country is looking for you," Catherine whispered to McBride, but to onlookers (even to Norbert and Khia), it looked like she was nuzzling up to him. "Do you know what they're saying about you?"

"Cut it out you two," Norbert protested, "There are children present."

McBride pulled Catherine closer, but she already knew what he was going to ask. "You want me to speak with her?"

McBride nodded.

†

As they were preparing to leave, Catherine gently suggested to Khia that they walk to the edge of a dry creek not far from the restaurant.

"Not easy being a foster kid is it? And taking care of your brother. It's a big responsibility."

Khia nodded, a little awestruck by this woman.

They talked for a while. What they talked about Norbert and McBride never did find out, but Khia came back … somehow … different. And some believe there are no such things as coincidences.

CHAPTER 10

The Weight and Width of a Ticket

A grain of sand will tip a scale,
a weak link will snap a chain,
the beat of a moth's wing ... inconsequential!
Really ... one better hope so.
Better yet, maybe you should pray.

The road trip unfolded without incident ... at least until they were pulled over.

As the police officer swaggered towards the truck, Norbert eyed Khia suspiciously. Would she say or do anything stupid?

"Ownership papers. Insurance," barked the officer, not taking off his opaque sunglasses.

The police officer reprimanded McBride for speeding and condescendingly warned him to drive more slowly in the future, especially with a couple of kids in the car. After issuing the ticket, he quickly waved them off and strutted pompously over to the next vehicle, which his partner had pulled over.

"Told you, you shouldn't have been going so fast," scowled Norbert.

McBride started the engine.

"What? Aren't you going to defend yourself? Tell me you weren't speeding," huffed Norbert.

"I wasn't," said McBride, looking concerned. He knew the Arizona license plate and his driver's license would be fed into the State computer. His fake driver's license would hold, but once the information was on the police database it could become a problem—a very big problem.

This one small traffic violation was like a grain of sand … a grain that tipped the scales, which had been, until that moment, weighted slightly in their favor—setting far away things in motion.

†

In a secure room, thousands of miles away, a team of Intelligence Officers had been briefed on an international pedophile ring that had abducted two children. They had no idea that the story was bogus or that their salaries were indirectly paid for by Blackwood Corporation. As instructed, they poured over mountains of data to glean anything useful. Powerful computers searched through international, national, state, and local databases, sifted through billions of credit card transactions, motor vehicle registrations, and police computer systems. Using complex algorithms, the sophisticated search engines cross-referenced information, looking for carefully chosen patterns and profiles.

An ordinary speeding ticket, like the beat of a butterfly's wing that caused a hurricane or a snowflake that triggered an avalanche, lit up a tiny red flag on Intelligence Officer Caro's computer screen, and beeped.

On any given day, hundreds, if not thousands, of red flags would light up the screens of hundreds of computers. It was painstaking work. Most were meaningless chatter but Intelligence Officer Caro was innately better than those around her.

Her finger poised on the delete button, she hesitated. Intrigued. The small piece of information, inputted into a police computer by a police officer with a faulty radar detector, made Officer Caro dig deeper. In her mind, she started putting together sequences and possibilities, digging even deeper, and shortly thereafter, she dutifully informed her superior.

"Good job, Caro," her supervisor commended her, placing his hand on her shoulder.

†

"I spy, with my little eye, something that is blue," said McBride.

"In the truck or out?" asked Devon excitedly.

Khia couldn't help but smile. She hadn't seen Devon this happy in a very long time. It was funny; instead of feeling trapped like she had at the beginning, being on the road had started to feel an awful lot like freedom.

"We've got company," announced McBride to Norbert. They had just passed a police car going in the opposite direction.

McBride watched in his rear-view mirror as the police cruiser did a 180, and put on their sirens. He answered Devon's question. "And it's inside the truck."

"The blue in the bottle?" asked Devon.

"You are gooooood," said McBride. "In one! Can you believe this kid? In one!"

Devon laughed.

They were a couple of miles south of the Canadian border. Agents Crawford and Azar had been heading west on a road that ran parallel to the interstate when they spotted their fourth two-tone blue pickup truck of the day.

"Didn't know there'd be so many two-tone blue pickup trucks," complained Crawford.

"Our shift ends in ten minutes," said Azar. "Let's skip it."

"The truck," said Crawford, in an exasperated voice. "We really should check it out."

"Ahrr, yeah ... you're right," moaned Azar.

Sirens blazing, Azar accelerated in pursuit of the pickup.

Crawford read the urgent notice aloud, "EXTREMELY DANGEROUS – two children, boy seven, girl fif ..."

"Why'd you stop reading?" Azar asked.

"Uh, the screen went blank," replied Crawford. He fiddled with the computer, hitting the machine with the flat of his hand trying to bring the information back.

"Haven't you memorized it yet? You read it aloud enough times ... or were you just practicing your reading?"

"We've got them! Train's coming. They'll have to stop at the railway crossing," commented Azar.

A hundred yards short of the railway crossing, the two-toned blue truck slowed. While the truck was still rolling, Azar watched as the passenger door popped open and a large man jumped out. His black leather coat swirled about him and a flash of silver caught Azar's eye, revealing a lethal-looking medieval sword.

Crawford, still messing with the computer and oblivious to the drama unfolding, heard his partner shout, "What the f—!"

Their world exploded. The roof of their car peeled away; dense, sharp steel missed their heads by a quarter of an inch, and glass showered them.

Azar knew he had reacted much too slowly, and then (by overcompensating) he reacted much too quickly. Gripping the steering wheel, he slammed on the brakes, causing the car to skid, bounce, and swerve ingloriously into the ditch. In slow-moving frames, their airbags exploded in their faces and bounced them back into normal time, shaken and disorientated.

Without question, Azar knew that he and his partner should have been dead. This guy with the sword was just messing with them.

Dazed and in the ditch, Azar looked up and saw the two-toned blue truck with its engine revving. The smoke cleared and revealed the passengers in the back seat: two kids, a girl and a boy, with their faces pressed to the window, looking keenly at the scene. Suddenly, standing by the driver's door, was a grinning man wearing a baseball cap and cheap pink sunglasses. He was holding a very real and powerful Uzi. But of equal importance (and perhaps of more immediate concern), was the large man in leather, only a few feet away, who was towering over them and still holding the big, sharp, silver sword.

"Hey we're cool man. Everything's good. Right?" said Crawford weakly.

"I want you to know we have kids too," spoke Azar.

"How about you shut up," ordered the man with the sword.

They fell silent.

"Your guns."

Crawford and Azar complied and slowly raised their arms and threw their weapons out the hole that was all that was left of where their window should have been.

"And cell phones."

The guy with the Uzi shouted, "Adios amigos! Pleasure meeting you!"

"One more thing," said the sword-bearer, as he crushed the cell phones with his boot. Jumping on the hood, he plunged his sword into the car as if he were slaying a dragon, destroying the dashboard and disabling their computer and communication equipment.

"Ciao," said the man with the sword, as he turned and hurled himself into the approaching truck.

"Norbert, I didn't know you spoke Italian," said McBride.

"It's a lot like Latin," replied Norbert.

With a squeal of tires, they crossed the railroad tracks and drove off.

Crawford and Azar, seasoned cops, got out of the car and stood in disbelief.

"Looks like they're headed for the border," commented Crawford.

"And how do you suppose they'll get across the border?" spat Azar.

"Those two kids look scared to you?" asked Crawford.

"No. Weird, isn't it?" replied Azar.

"Shouldn't we try to call in what just happened?" asked Crawford.

"With what?" snapped Azar.

"How the hell are we going to explain this to the chief?" asked Azar, who had turned and looked dejectedly at their wrecked vehicle.

"The truth," offered Crawford weakly.

"Are you kidding? We'll have to make something up; she'll never believe this."

†

Pulling up to the window of the Custom's Officer at the International border, McBride and Norbert were prepared for evasive action. Call it a miracle, some kind of divine intervention, but the computer systems that automatically scanned vehicle license plates and VIN numbers, whose cameras automatically identified drivers with facial recognition systems, and whose detectors listened for electromagnetic signatures and monitored for unusual amounts of radioactive gamma and delta waves, were down.

At the risk of traffic backing up for hours, the overworked customs agents were doing their job the old-fashion way: asking questions and looking for suspicious activity.

The border guard asked the typical questions about the purpose of their visit, whether they had anything to declare, their expected date of return, and then unexpectedly leaned into the truck and asked Khia, "What is your relationship to these two men?"

Without hesitation, Khia flashed the officer a sweet shy smile and politely answered, "Sir, these are my two uncles. They're taking us to our grandmother's."

The border guard who was trained to look for anomalies, for terrorists, child abductors, illegal activities, as well as the importation of illegal fruits and vegetables, also knew how to read for signs of anxiety and stress, but he was a bit of an old softy when it came to polite, well-behaved children. There were so few of them around these days! After a cursory look at their documents, he waved them on with a smile, "Welcome to Canada."

†

Ten minutes later, the computers flashed on. An urgent message burst across the border guards' computer screens, making one of them feel suddenly very, very ill.

The net that the Blackwood Corporation had created was closing in, but they had somehow slipped through.

CHAPTER 11

Into the Dark
Dark Forest

Crossing over eased the tension … but only somewhat.

"I thought we were supposed to be going to New York City?" asked Khia.

"We are," answered McBride, scrunching his face. "But first we … uh, Norbert and I … we think it's prudent to take a detour. That is, we … uh … we are going to see an old friend in the Northern lands. I think you'll like her; she's uh different, in an odd …" McBride searched for the right words, "lovable, in an eccentric kind of way."

Norbert stepped in, "You're finally at a loss for words, McBride? What he means to say is," he looked at Khia, "you'll like Nora."

†

Avoiding major roads and highways, they maintained an almost invisible profile on dirt and gravel roads—roads that weren't labeled on any official map or satellite guidance system.

Their last gas up was one of the most worrisome parts of the journey. Stopping at a self-serve gas station, the kids hid in the backseat under blankets, surrounded by boxes and supplies.

McBride filled up the gas tank, as well as several spare red fuel containers, while Norbert ordered a super-supper-sized take-out for two at the diner.

Paying cash, it wasn't long before they were on the road again. Pulling away, they turned down a lonely country road, narrowly missing the police car that cruised into the gas station.

"You've done good," Norbert praised Khia and Devon, as they burst out of their hiding place.

"Seatbelts on, kids," McBride shouted. "Safety first."

McBride struck a course northward into the forested interior. Khia was enthralled. Never having been so far north, she half expected the temperature to drop significantly and to see snow falling from the sky. Khia had never seen snow before and probably wouldn't see snow this time around either. It was too early in the season. Unusually hot and dry, the entire continent had suffered from an extended heat wave and drought. There were ominous signs in the dry brittle forest. A single match carelessly tossed out a window could easily cause a forest fire. But if not for the drought causing water levels to be unusually low, they would never have crossed the river or attempted to cross the gorge.

"Whoa," Norbert shouted, at the same time as McBride stepped on the brakes, skidding to a full stop.

At first glance, it seemed inadvisable to attempt the crossing, but it would be a shortcut. After Norbert checked the depth of the water, a course was set and they boldly drove on. Despite tires skidding on the slick, slimy river rocks, and water entering the cab at its deepest, the truck forded its way across to the dry shore.

It was later that they faced their greatest challenge: a deep gully. It was long, narrow, and steep. It looked something like the Greek letter omega 'Ω', but upside down. Khia was sure that this time they'd have to turn back and find another way. Sometimes shortcuts end up costing you more time, but sometimes it works in your favor and it's exactly where you are supposed to be.

Unperturbed, McBride studied the natural impediment. He bent down to take a closer look, squinted his eyes. He even held a fistful of dry earth and let it fall slowly from his hand seeing what affect the nonexistent breeze might have; weighing every little thing to the smallest degree. "We're moving forward," he finally announced. "Get out."

Norbert, Khia and Devon scrambled down into the gorge and climbed up the other side. McBride revved the engine preparing for the crossing.

As they waited and watched apprehensively, Norbert whispered confidingly to his two young charges, "If anyone can do it, it's McBride."

McBride stepped on the accelerator, knowing that he had only one chance. If the vehicle got stuck, there would be little chance to get it out and they'd be faced with an incredibly long journey, through rocky inhospitable terrain, on foot—the truck left to rust and be reclaimed by the earth.

McBride maneuvered the vehicle expertly, controlling the degrees and angles, and went down into the gully. Dust and earth flew into the air as he gunned the vehicle to get the crucial momentum needed for the upgrade.

On the edge, it hit its apex. The vehicle hung motionless in the air. It could have tipped sideways, lurched over onto its roof, or rolled back into the gully, but slowly … by the force of gravity … like the winged beat of a butterfly or a single snowflake's fall that causes an avalanche, the scales tipped and the truck landed hard but safely onto the narrow path on the other side.

Devon jumped up and down screaming and clapping with excitement and even Khia found herself joining in.

Standing by the vehicle, McBride grinned his patented grin, as Devon ran over and took a flying leap into his arms to give him the biggest bear hug ever.

Norbert gave McBride a noncommittal nod. "Thought we'd be walking."

†

The radio played softly. As they drove deeper into the wilderness, the FM and then the AM radio signals were replaced with disjointed static. By eleven o'clock, only one station weakly sent out its sporadic signal. The station played jazz and serenaded them into the night, until it too gave off only unintelligible noise. Norbert leaned forward and switched off the radio. They were left with the hum of the truck, the eerie silence of the wilderness, and the fuel gage getting lower and lower.

Into the dark, dark forest, with the dashboard lights illuminating the interior of the cab, no one said anything until Norbert asked, "McBride, how come you didn't get satellite radio?"

"At the prices they were asking?" answered McBride.

Norbert accepted his answer, but in about half an hour, broke the silent darkness with his late response, "You could have haggled with them."

"I wouldn't want to take advantage of Ms Percival's generosity, now would I?" asked McBride with a glint in his eyes.

†

With the last of their spare fuel in the truck's tank, their food supply low, and water the same temperature as the ambient air, Norbert again broke the silence and said, "We should have been there by now."

"I'm looking for the hidden entrance," replied McBride. "Everything's changed. Last time, this place hadn't yet recovered from the clear cutting. A lot has grown back."

McBride slowed the truck and came to a stop. He put the truck into reverse and backed up a few yards. Two ancient gnarled trees had wrapped themselves around solid rock; they had found their entrance.

Khia woke up as Norbert was lifting two great tree branches that hid a road, if you could call it that—the dirt road was barely the width of the truck.

They covered another twenty miles. The truck clipped branches and brambles along its sides until it emerged near the top of a moderate-sized ridge.

Looking down, Khia saw a small protected valley. It looked magical, almost as if it didn't belong. But it was there: a globe of light coming from a house nestled in the vast dark wilderness. The light beckoned to her, attracting her to the needed respite from their long journey.

†

Earlier that evening, in the White Hills, the Brislings were settling in for the night.

The two older girls were out and Mr. Brisling, tired from a busy day of *honey-do-jobs*, was slumped fast asleep on his recliner. Mrs. Brisling was in the kitchen, preparing things for the coming day, and the family dog was agitated ... whining and scratching at the front door. This was happening a lot recently. Mrs. Brisling reprimanded the dog in an overly harsh tone. Though the dog was cowed, it continued growling and pawing at the door.

Exasperated, Mrs. Brisling opened the door, but she could see nothing. She walked out onto the porch, her fingertips lightly holding the door open for the dog to come out. The dog, half in and half out, cocked its head to one side and sniffed the turbulent air. Strong gusts of wind swirled about the street. The streetlights came on, giving the neighborhood an in-between feeling of something being not quite right.

"Come on, Rosie," encouraged Mrs. Brisling, but the canine backed her way into the house whimpering.

Across the street, a few streetlights away, one of the lights went out, its filament overheated; it had broken its electrical contact, making the neighborhood noticeably darker.

Stepping back inside the house, Mrs. Brisling quickly locked the door, and set the deadbolt into place.

"Audrey," she called to her youngest. "It's well past your bedtime. I hope you're brushing your teeth."

Audrey felt a cold breeze.

Curious, with a toothbrush in her hand, she walked down the corridor to the room that Devon had used.

The door that should have been closed was slightly ajar.

Slowly, she pushed the door open and walked inside. It was dark. Reaching up on tiptoe, she turned on the light. The window was wide open and the curtains were moving wildly in the wind.

Audrey walked to the window and leaned out, but a sound in the room caused her to jump and turn.

"Devon!" squealed Audrey, pleased that her playmate had returned. "I missed you, where have you been?"

But Devon didn't say anything; he just looked at her with his large eyes and white teeth.

Audrey laughed delightedly, "Would you like to play with me? Stay here. I'll get my dolls and we can play house. I'll let you play with the horse." Audrey skipped down the corridor to get her toys.

†

A deep cold shiver ran through Mrs. Brisling like a dark premonition. Something … was … wrong. "Audrey?" she called again.

But there was no answer.

"Audrey?" she repeated more loudly, starting to make her way to the stairs—her throat feeling suddenly dry.

The entire week had been quite out of the ordinary, what with the church fire, Khia and Devon's sudden departure, and those two strange men with government identification cards who had shown up the other day asking all sorts of questions.

They had arrived while she had been vacuuming. She had glanced out the window and noticed her middle daughter, Snowden, talking to the two men. Turning the vacuum off, the house felt unusually silent, as she went out to confront the two men and her daughter. Snowden should have been old enough to know better than to talk to strangers.

"Hello Mrs. Brisling," spoke one of the men, anticipating her approach. "Can I call you Polly?" he asked, turning his head as she stepped beside him.

She hated being called Polly.

He smiled, but it wasn't a very nice smile. "My name is Agent Burdock and this is Cocklebur," he said, by way of an introduction. "If you have time, and I'm sure you do, we would like to ask you a few questions—questions about the whereabouts of two children recently in your care: Khia and Devon."

"Your daughter," his partner reached over to the young girl and stroked her hair, which caused Mrs. Brisling to feel a surge of uneasy queasiness in her stomach, with equal parts of fear rising up her spine, "has been of immense help to us."

She suspected that her daughter Snowden had already divulged everything she knew about Khia and Devon, and that she had likely embellished
what she hadn't known. Mrs. Brisling also sensed the implicit warning that
wasn't spoken, too subtle for Snowden. "What is it you want to know?"
asked Mrs. Brisling coldly.

"Where are the Ashworths?"

"I don't know where they are, Mr. Burdock; that is your name, isn't it?"
He made no acknowledgment. At this point, she was getting confused as
to which was which—Cocklebur or Burdock. They both looked intimidating with their tall bulk and muscles and short-cropped hair. Mrs. Brisling
started to ramble. "I haven't seen them in days; I think they must have
run off during all the commotion. Our church," her voice caught, "our
church, you know ... burnt down."

Cocklebur stroked her daughter's hair again, and then placed his hand
on her shoulder.

Snowden's feelings of empowerment evaporated.

Fortunately, at that moment, Mr. Brisling had pulled into the driveway—not that he was any match for the two men.

He got out of the minivan, concern written on his face when he saw
the unmistakable look of fear in his wife's eyes.

Cocklebur winked at Snowden and stepped into the black car with its
black-tinted windows.

Burdock sank down on one knee, as if he were proposing to the young
girl in front of her parents. Snowden had provided them with all the information they had needed, "Thank you for your help today; perhaps one
day we will meet again, little lady."

Getting up, he turned to Mrs. Brisling, "Thank you ma'am," he said
politely, but his eyes were cold and hard. "Your help has been greatly
appreciated. If you remember anything more that could be of help to us
in our investigation, here's my card. Call me."

Mrs. Brisling tried to shake off the growing uncomfortable feeling
within her.

"Audrey," she called out, as she made her way, step by step, up to the
top of the stairs, "I hope you're brushing your teeth."

The door to what had been Devon's room cast its shadowed light into the darkened hallway.

"Audrey, you better not be in there," she said firmly.

The cold breeze whipped around her. "I told you not to go into that room." She peered in and saw her youngest daughter standing by the bed.

Mrs. Brisling sighed and leaned up against the door frame, relieved and reprimanding herself for her silly thoughts, "Audrey, come on dear, it's bedtime."

So it came as a nasty, sickening shock to Mrs. Brisling when she turned around and saw her daughter skipping along the corridor with an armful of toys, making her way towards the room.

"Devon's back. We're going to play," said Audrey excitedly.

Mrs. Brisling turned a pasty white and her knees felt weak. She raised her arm, stopping Audrey. Toys fell to the floor.

Mrs. Brisling looked back into the room, afraid of what she might see.

But the room was empty.

The only movement came from the curtains that fluttered in the gusting wind. Her body trembled as she told Audrey to go to her room. Methodically, she checked the room. She opened the closet door and looked under the bed. With trembling hands, she shut the bedroom window and smoothed the curtains. Leaving the room, she turned off the light and closed the door behind her.

Going to her daughter, she held her very tightly.

CHAPTER 12

A Home in the Wilderness

A lifetime lived with cats and dogs
Is a lifetime well lived.

"It's been a long time, McBride," a husky voice came from inside the cabin. The tone softened but only a little, "What took you so long? I've been expecting you for hours."

"How did you know we were coming?" asked McBride.

"I have my ways," said Nora. The Ojibwa woman stood at the door frame of her house, silhouetted by the white light and hues of reds and warm wood tones. "Well, come on in."

They quickly scurried in and closed the door behind them in an effort to keep out the large moths that were attracted to the light. It took a moment for Khia's eyes to adjust to the bright light in the cabin. Nora's log home looked bigger on the inside. It was made of large round logs, some more than a foot in diameter, and a big stone fireplace in the living room. It was warm and comforting—a place that instantly felt like home.

Nora's place was bursting with old books, maps, and Indian quilts. There were all sorts of things you'd expect to find in a remote cabin in the woods, where one had to be resourceful and self-sufficient. There were shelves with weird stuff on them, like dried herbs hanging on small hooks and various jars with different things being preserved. The place exuded a broth of rich intoxicating aromas.

But there were also things you would not imagine belonging to a place so far from the city. Nora had a shiny new stainless steel refrigerator and an amazing AGA stove. Khia heard the distinctive sound of a washing machine in spin mode behind a closed door. In the corner, a laptop computer displayed its screen saver: a bistro with a table with four wineglasses, filled with rich red wine, and crusty bread.

"The beds are made. Norbert and McBride, one of you will have to use the den, the other the pullout in the living room; the kids can sleep in the spare room. I've got the tea steeping."

Two good-natured dogs pushed open a door and ran up to Khia, almost bowling her over; she started petting them and their tails wagged furiously.

Carrying a sleeping Devon, Norbert navigated his way to the bedroom and gently laid him down on one of the twin beds. Khia, with the dogs following, went to help. Khia removed his shoes and gently covered him with a thick handmade quilt. Devon cooed in approval, much more asleep than awake.

As Khia and Norbert returned, Khia caught the disapproving, quizzical expression on the Indian woman's face, "On another one of your assignments?"

McBride looked sheepishly at her.

"Oh wait. Let me guess, in trouble again," she continued sarcastically. "Up against impossible odds and you need my help? And you and your friends want to stay here a couple of days so that you can come up with a better plan. Am I right?"

McBride nodded and smiled sweetly, "Yup."

"How do you know these things?" asked Norbert.

"You, of all people should ask?" she looked unforgivingly at the large man.

"What! You've always amazed me," answered Norbert.

Nora laughed; it was a sound that was rich and inviting. "Although I'm sorely tempted, I have never turned away friends."

Khia heaved a sigh of relief and then realized that the woman had been teasing them.

McBride laughed out loud, stepped forward, and hugged her, "Good to see you too, Nora."

Nora whispered in his ear, "Evil is coming. It is nearing."

Khia strained but couldn't hear what was said.

Stepping away from McBride, Nora cocked her head to one side, as if listening to something no one else could hear. She shook her head, as if dispelling whatever it was she had seen, or felt. "We have time."

Turning her attention on Norbert, she said, "You haven't changed a bit, except for the scar." She traced her fingers along its jagged length.

Norbert, who rarely smiled, gave Nora a grin. "Makes me look more handsome, but you, you old witch ... you've got more meat on your bones and you're grayer than the last time I saw you, and also ..." he paused and gave her the once over, squinting his eyes, "uh, yep, and maybe a little shorter too."

Khia cringed.

"Come here and give me a hug," Nora said, not in the least bit offended. Norbert picked her up easily off the ground, and moved her around in a few slow circles before planting her back on her feet.

Nora turned to Khia, "A young girl with these two angels of deception who bend the rules so ... creatively. The world must indeed be in a desperate situation. Hello Khia. My name is Nora."

"Hello," said Khia. "We're going to visit our grandmother," she blurted, feeling like she had to say something.

"Yes, I know," Nora replied kindly.

"Khia," Nora mulled over her name. "You have a powerful name. Your mother named you well."

Wanting attention, the two dogs started barking. "I see you've met Zip and Zipper. While you're here, would you like the task of feeding them?"

Khia nodded enthusiastically.

Placing her hands on her hips, Nora looked at McBride and Norbert, "And nobody, I repeat nobody, stays in my home without contributing something."

"Nora, Nora, Nora ..." smiled McBride.

"Uh," she lifted her finger to shush him, turned to Khia, and said, "My dogs get fed once a day, in the morning."

With wide serious eyes, Khia nodded, knowing that she did not want to disappoint this woman.

"These two rotten dogs of mine," continued Nora, "may get fed once a day, but they're allowed treats. If you want, you'll find the dog treats in the kitchen cupboard under the sink."

At the sound of the word '*treats*', the two dogs wagged their tails even more vigorously, moving in excited circles. Khia made her way to the kitchen. Fighting over their backs and thick whacking tails, she found the doggie biscuits and giggled a little, as she tried to avoid the dogs' wet noses and tongues.

Followed by the two dogs, Khia joined the three adults, who had already seated themselves in the living room. Khia listened to the banter—stories that brought about genuine sounds of laughter and an occasional tear. Khia, fascinated by their stories, wanted to stay awake but couldn't fight sleep any longer.

"Time to get some sleep," said Nora.

Settling in-between the crisp sheets, Khia breathed deeply; the blankets smelled of pine and deep forest, having been dried on an outdoor clothesline. Devon was fast asleep in the other bed. Zip and Zipper lay at the foot of his bed, and before long, a small black cat snuggled up to her—its purring like a serenade. Khia closed her eyes.

Nora stood quietly at the doorway. She saw the dark smudges under the young girl's eyes, "Rest child," she said empathically. "A dreamless sleep tonight."

Khia was asleep so fast that she didn't hear the words Nora spoke over her like a protective spell.

CHAPTER 13

A World Without Light

And then there was light ...

Khia's eyes fluttered open. It had been the deepest sleep she had had in, like, forever. Allowing herself a huge satisfying stretch, she looked around the room and everything was strange and unfamiliar. Where was she? She had that feeling again—of being in that in-between place of not being asleep but not being completely awake either.

Then the memories of the past few days flooded back, "Oh no," she cried, and scrambled out of bed. She was supposed to feed the dogs.

She heard Devon's laughter and made her way to the living room. Devon was wrestling with Norbert, thinking he had the upper hand against his larger opponent.

"Grab him in a headlock," called out McBride, who stood on the sidelines encouraging the young boy. "I wouldn't take that if I were you ... yeah, yeah, poke him in the eyes."

The sound of the screen door brought all their activity to a sudden stop. Nora stood at the doorway. Zip and Zipper walked in and went to their mats.

"You slept well?" Nora asked.

Khia nodded.

"Khia, you're to come with me today," said Nora. The Indian woman turned her attention on Norbert, McBride, and Devon. She narrowed her eyes, folding her arms over her chest, "I expect my house to be near immaculate when I return. Norbert, firewood needs to be cut. Devon, watch out for bears, and McBride, do what you do best. Get dressed Khia, and have some breakfast; the dogs have been fed. We'll be leaving shortly."

Uh oh, thought Khia.

In less than twenty minutes, Khia had finished her breakfast, and dressed in jeans and a purple T-shirt, and her new jacket and hiking boots.

Without waiting or saying anything, Nora picked up her knapsack, and left the house.

Khia was unsure what to do. She looked at McBride, then at Norbert, and then back at McBride. They gave her pained expressions; McBride's was more like a half smile, and Norbert's more of a grimace, both motioning her to follow Nora.

The screen door banged loudly and Khia ran to catch up to the older Indian woman.

They watched until Khia disappeared from sight.

"Hope she's going to be all right," said McBride.

"Ahhh, she'll be fine," Norbert said, dismissively. Then he chuckled, "At least I have the guy job. Oh, and McBride, don't forget to vacuum under the couch, and for lunch, something hot ... not cold sandwiches."

"Shut up, Norbert," was McBride's good-natured retort, but his voice quickly changed to one of concern. "What do you think? You think the girl trusts us now?"

Norbert shrugged his shoulders. "Why should she?" he asked seriously.

"Do you think she's too young?" asked McBride.

"Yup," answered Norbert.

"Do you think Nora can help Khia?" asked McBride.

"Yup," repeated Norbert.

"Do you think—?"

"McBride," Norbert interrupted him, before he could ask another question he couldn't answer. "You're irritating me. Your problem is you worry too much. Khia has us. What more does she need?"

Norbert's attention was drawn to Devon, who had begun wrestling with the dogs in the living room. The dogs, as big as Devon, didn't seem to mind the abuse a seven year old could wreak on them.

Devon threw a sopping wet ball across the room. Excitedly, the dogs chased it, knocking and jostling everything in their path. A glass vase crashed to the floor and shattered.

"Devon! Front and center!" Norbert yelled, a little too harshly. Norbert, who wasn't always aware of his own strength, also wasn't always aware of the impact the sound of his booming voice had on others.

Devon looked abashed, knowing he shouldn't have thrown the ball in the house.

Norbert gave the boy his marching orders while leading him outside, handed him a shovel that was bigger than him, and told him to push the rusted red wagon to the compost heap.

"Don't forget to watch out for bears; you'd make a delicious snack between meals. And remember, if you see a bear, no running. Hit it on the nose with your shovel and do not—I repeat, DO NOT—call for help unless it's an absolute emergency."

Devon looked up at him, his eyes quite large. Cautiously, the young boy struggled with his chores. Every now and then he peered into the forest, looking for bears.

"Don't worry kid, I'll send McBride out if you have a problem," Norbert shouted, as he struck a log with the ax, easily splitting it in two. Carrying an armful of logs into the house, he left Devon alone.

Norbert poured himself a cup of coffee and called out conspiratorially to McBride, "Hey McBride! Do you think it would be funny if—?"

"No," announced McBride, horrified, knowing exactly what his friend had in mind. "You've already scared him enough."

"Come on," insisted Norbert. "The kid can handle it. He'll laugh about it when he's older."

"No!" said McBride more sternly, shaking his head. "The kid's only seven. It would scare the poop out of him."

"Ah, you're no fun, McBride," said Norbert, contemptuously. But despite his rough and somewhat playful antics, Norbert kept a watchful eye on his young charge and the forest beyond.

†

For the umpteenth time, McBride checked the evening meal; why he bothered made no sense, because it had dried out hours ago.

At last, the screen door creaked open, and banged shut, announcing their return. Khia dragged her tired blistered feet and sat at the kitchen table.

McBride turned to look at Nora. He was taken aback; he'd never seen her this way before. She looked worried. Deep lines etched her face. It was like she'd aged a year in a single day.

"You must be hungry," McBride said, as he served the burnt offerings.

While the two ate, Norbert and McBride waited, itching to know what had happened. Unable to handle the silence any longer, Norbert got up and turned on the radio, brought in by satellite, but he froze when he heard Khia and Devon's names.

...two American children, Khia Aleyne and Devon Ashworth, abducted from the steps of a burning church, are believed to be in Canada. Border officials are blaming a computer glitch but are unable to explain how their security systems could have failed at such a critical juncture. A wide search is being conducted with American and Canadian authorities. The abductors are considered armed and dangerous. Unconfirmed reports indicate a violent altercation took place with the killing of two American officials in Northern Minnesota near the Canadian border. Sources suspect the child abductors are part of an international pedophile ring. Police are asking that if anyone has any information they are to contact this number...

In disgust, Norbert turned off the radio. "So, we're murders and child abductors now," he spat out angrily.

An unnatural and foreboding silence enveloped the cabin.

Nora quietly finished her meal before she spoke. "Someone's gone to great lengths to restrict your movements."

She stood up and went to the living room; Norbert followed, leaving McBride with Khia.

As he was cleaning up the kitchen, McBride ventured some carefully chosen words. "Well kid, how was your day? Better than mine, I hope."

Khia smiled noncommittally.

"Let's go outside," prompted McBride.

It was a luminous night, with not a cloud in the sky; tens of thousands of stars brilliantly shone over their heads.

After some time, Khia finally spoke.

†

...The screen door banged loudly and Khia ran to catch up to Nora, who was already disappearing into the dark forest.

Walking for hours, Khia had lost track of time. Stopping at a natural spring, Khia thirstily drank the cool refreshing water while Nora filled a small leather flask.

They continued their trek. In new hiking boots, Khia's feet were blistered and her legs were feeling the strain of the upward climb.

The sun was well passed its zenith. Khia watched as the shadows expanded into the gorge. She saw something skittering away and she thought of that day in the alley with the bag lady.

Nora pointed up to a ledge on the cliff face. Khia's eyes were drawn to the site; it was impossible to miss, because the entire gorge was cast in shadow except for the small ledge drenched in sunlight. As they climbed higher, the ground became steeper and sparser of vegetation.

Without complaint, Khia pushed herself along, following Nora up the steep path that had been carved out of the escarpment by wind, rain, and ice. When she reached the ledge, the panoramic view was mesmerizing, and so much wilder and grander than she could have ever imagined.

"My ancestors," spoke Nora, looking at the vast expanse, "used to think this place was holy. But like so many things Indian, this place has been almost forgotten."

Khia looked around and saw that, at the back of the ledge, there was a shallow cave sheltered in ancient metamorphic rock, with a diagonal band of rose quartz cut across the rock face.

Khia followed Nora into the cave. The walls and floors were painted with ancient symbols and drawings. Carved in the rock floor was an elaborate mandala, which Nora explained represented creation. It was quite beautiful. Khia could feel the energy.

"Why am I here?" asked Khia.

"To find your way," replied Nora, walking to the center of the cave. It was surprisingly warm and beautiful in the diffused afternoon sunlight.

"I don't understand," said Khia.

"Are you prepared to learn?" asked Nora.

"Yes."

Nora spread out two blankets on the rock floor and sat down crossed-legged on one. She motioned for Khia to sit and Khia mirrored her.

"Where we are going there is nothing that you will understand as normal. Are you ready to take your first step?" asked Nora.

"I ... I think so," Khia responded hesitantly.

"Normally I would wait until you were a few years older." She looked at her sadly. "Sometimes sacrifices have to be made, required from the very old and sometimes from the very young. You need not be afraid. I will be right here with you for as long as you need me."

Nora took out the flask that she had filled earlier from the spring and poured some water into a shallow indention in the red rock. On contact, the water hissed. The stone was inexplicably hot and most of the liquid evaporated, leaving a dry white stain.

With two fingers of her right hand, Nora dipped her hand in the small amount of remaining water, touched Khia's forehead, lips, and heart, and whispered as if in a prayer, "Hidden right in front of your eyes."

Her touch was warm—almost hot. Khia felt a little light-headed and closed her eyes. She heard Nora's voice, strangely far away and fading. "Hidden right in front of your eyes."

In her mind, Khia repeated Nora's words like an ancient mantra that reverberated within her ... *Hidden ... hidden right in front of your eyes.*

†

It was well past the witching hour when Meg found the courage to return to the alley. With effort, she had righted her grocery cart and slowly picked up her scattered possessions. When she saw the staff, broken in two and lifeless, gray tears fell from her old eyes. She held the two pieces of the staff close to her chest, cradling it like a stillborn baby in her arms. Unsteadily, she shuffled from the alley, one hand gripping her broken staff and the other pushing the grocery cart, with one of its wheels screeching loudly.

Haunting images (vague memories of her past) flashed through her mind: images of a once idyllic life ripped from her, of pain, of torture ... Once before she had been separated from her staff; she knew, but couldn't quite remember ... snapshots of digging through coarse green grass, into dark soil, and through a layer of black ash to find her staff buried in the earth.

Kneeling under the bridge, the place she had retreated to, she gazed upon her broken staff. Confused, she didn't know where she was, or what to do; she was lost.

And then, an amazing thing started to happen. The two pieces of her staff began to glow faintly ... and as the glow grew stronger so a faint unnamed hope grew within Meg. The blue white glow became blindingly bright. Her hands shaking with the effort, she aligned the two pieces of her staff.

As the space between the two pieces came together, an array of colors, brilliant whites, and diffused hues of electric blues filled the space under the bridge. There was a terrific crack and a surge of energy that threw Meg backwards.

The staff fell to the ground—once again whole.

The clear blue light faded, leaving only darkness.

Meg lay on the ground, momentarily blinded by the bright light and the sudden return to darkness. Struggling to get onto her hands and knees, she reached out, feeling for her staff. When she found it, she grasped it tightly, never wanting to let it go. With its help and support, she stood up, and it was then, in that moment, that Meg remembered someone. Her name was ... Val ... Valerie. But just as quickly as it was remembered, the name was forgotten as if it had never been. And not knowing why ... Meg struck the ground, slowly and deliberately, three times ... as if knocking against a heavy door.

†

At first Khia didn't notice anything odd or unusual. In fact, she felt a little foolish, and like many girls her age, got a little fidgety. Then she got a little bored, and started to get a little annoyed. This was stupid.

"Khia," she heard Nora's voice, sounding very far away, "you can open your eyes."

Khia slowly opened her eyes. Everything around her had changed. Instead of being in a dimly lit cave and there being a spectacular view of the wilderness, in its changing montage of autumn colors, everything was black and incredibly silent. She wasn't even sure her eyes were open.

Khia had never experienced anything like this before. In the city, even in the deadest of nights and in the darkest of alleys, there was always some light and some sound. But here, there was nothing, absolute silence, no wind, not even the sound of the high and low-pitched frequencies found almost everywhere on the earth (a sound that, if you stopped right now, you would hear).

"Nora," Khia asked in a tight whisper, "are you here with me?"

"I am."

Khia was relieved to hear Nora's voice, yet it came from no discernible direction, seemingly emanating from all around. "You cannot see me, but I am here," she said reassuringly.

"What is this place?" asked Khia, intrigued.

"We are nowhere and everywhere. Like all places and times, it is a place that simply is," answered Nora.

Nora's words had a soothing effect on Khia. A light laugh escaped her lips. It was a sound that brought a soft stirring to the place. *Wow, this is cool,* she thought.

"Very good Khia, you discern well. You have passed your first test. Getting here is a feat very few manage, especially on their first try. I must, however, set a new task before you. It is, let us say … more difficult … for it is its opposite. Trust. Trust in yourself, which is something we all must learn."

Khia listened attentively.

"Find your way out," Nora's voice faded into the all-encompassing silent blackness.

"That's it?" asked Khia, expecting more instruction. "Nora?"

But Nora was gone.

The shock of being left alone in the world of darkness sunk in and it made Khia angry and afraid. Nora had said she'd be by her side as long as she needed her … but where was she?

"Nora!" she screamed.

Frightened, and not knowing what to do, Khia got up and walked around, trying to release some nervous energy and quell her rising panic.

She felt like running, but not being able to see where she was going, she was afraid that maybe she'd fall into a void or something and never get out.

She had to think.

Trying to slow her breathing, she took a few deep breaths. It helped to calm her nerves. *I can will myself back*, she thought. Except, absolutely nothing happened. She was still here.

Panic threatened to return, but she took another deep breath. Nora's words returned. *Trust in yourself.*

Okay, thought Khia, *Nora said it would be harder, but it was possible.* It was its opposite. But how had they gotten here? She wasn't sure. In her mind, Khia went back to her starting position and recited her original mantra. *Hidden right in front of your eyes.* But she couldn't see anything.

She tried sitting like a Tibetan-Buddhist monk in meditation, but that didn't work. She knelt and prayed to the Almighty. Nothing happened.

Then she stood, clicked her heels together three times, and said (really, really meaning it), "There's no place like home; there's no place like home."

That didn't work either, not that she had expected it to. She laughed a little, and with the laughter something changed.

That was when she saw it, slowly moving towards her. It was a disturbance, barely noticeable but unmistakably there. Elation infused her; she closed her eyes, and the chatter inside her head was gone. She felt it. It felt like a sea wave lifting her up and ever so gently setting her down on a warm and sandy beach.

Where it had come from she didn't know, but it didn't matter, for suddenly she knew the answer. It was as if she had always known. The knowledge came bubbling from deep within her, and a delightful, unexpected laugh escaped her. And Khia knew she could get back.

Khia opened her eyes. The Dark World wasn't dark at all; it was, in fact, teeming with energy coming in and out of existence in a seemingly chaotic jumble of possibilities, but there were patterns within patterns—a balance and symmetry that she'd never noticed before.

And then, a moment later, she was hovering between the world of light and the so-called world of dark that Nora had brought her to and left her in. It was beautiful, and she was juxtaposed between worlds—betwixt and between ... between and betwixt.

CHAPTER 14

Timothea

Neither here nor there, Khia hovered over the so-called real world. She saw her physical body, locked in a trance, sitting with her legs crossed. Nora was leaning against the cave wall and seemed to look right through her. It was like she could sense her but couldn't see her. Euphoria filled Khia. She had done it. She had passed the second test. This was so cool. Acting on impulse, she returned to the Dark World so that she could bounce back and forth, into and between both realms. She did this even though a small voice inside her head said, '*You better not!*'

She didn't listen to it.

She was feeling elated and very pleased with herself, and wanted the feeling to go on a little longer.

In the Dark World, just when Khia had decided to return to Nora, she saw (or thought she saw) a flash of light. It was far in the opaque distance. She took a step towards it, and then another and another.

She stopped.

Everything was still and dark.

Doubts began to surface. Had she simply imagined it? She stood perfectly still and waited. Was this another part of Nora's lesson? As she started to give up on the light, it flickered on again ... much brighter this time.

So, she hadn't imagined it. But where was it coming from? It was so near, yet so far away. She wanted to know.

With no reference point, there was no way of telling if she was getting closer to the light or farther away. For that matter, there was no way of telling if the light itself was moving towards her or away from her. Either way, intermittent flashes of light became a beacon forming a small steady pale blue glow.

And then the light leapt into the air like a bauble of pale blue light, shining as bright as the northern star, guiding her way.

A few inches from the boundary, Khia stood where the light had been separated from the dark. The atmosphere was so delicate that her breath disturbed the filmy surface, causing multicolored, irregular, shimmering lines to ripple out. And then she saw what lay beyond. It was a world within a world … like looking through a child's glass globe with a magical world inside.

Khia blinked a few times to make sure she was really seeing what she was seeing. There was a great castle in the air. A ring of clouds at its base made it look suspended, but it actually rested atop a rocky hill. As she walked nearer, she saw that there was a moat, a drawbridge, and turrets—the kind you would find in a fairy story. Not able to resist such an enchanted place, Khia tentatively stepped over the threshold.

As soon as she stepped into this world, everything changed. A thick shroud of cloud, with tinges of silver and turquoise, enveloped her. She could barely see the sun; even so, she knew it was much smaller and much closer than the earth's sun, giving little light or warmth. And most noticeably, the land was dull and limp. She felt its sadness.

Starting to feel a little anxious, Khia had just decided that it was best to leave when she heard snippets of sound. It was the most divine sound, yet utterly heartbreaking … and it was drawing her in.

Khia made her way towards the castle. Lingering on the bridge a moment, she looked down and saw that the moat was dry and the earth was cracked. Despite her trepidation, she was unable to ignore the lamenting sound and walked through the open gate, under the portcullis, and into the courtyard.

As she did so, the world inside the bauble of light grew brighter, warmer, and felt more alive. Inviting her in, a gentle sweet breeze touched her skin as lightly as a kiss.

In the courtyard, the sound seemed to float all around, making it impossible to tell where the sad sound was coming from.

Moving towards a large archway, Khia entered a spectacular garden. The life in the garden was a crescendo of sounds, colors, and vibrant scents. The bower was in full bloom. In this oasis, there was an indescribable amount of energy. Water cascaded from silver fountains, flowers burst open, trees rustled in the playful breeze, and butterflies fluttered about under a brilliant azure sky that held the golden youthful sun. It was breathtakingly beautiful.

Sitting under a cluster of great trees that seemed to bow their crowns to her, there was a lone figure—the vocalist. A silver wolf lay protectively at her feet, and at her fingertips perched a black bird.

Khia didn't move. Afraid she might break the spell, she waited, enraptured by the woman's clear-pitched voice.

The woman's song came to an end, leaving Khia feeling somehow empty and alone, and wishing desperately that she hadn't stopped singing. The lady turned her head slightly to one side, as if she were at last aware of Khia's presence. The singer, draped in a turquoise and silver gown, rose elegantly to her feet. The wolf loped towards Khia and the black bird launched itself into the air and cawed, "Khiaaaa, Khiaaa."

The black bird settled on Khia's outstretched hand and the silver wolf allowed her to stroke its thick soft fur.

Of course, Khia immediately recognized them. She knew that they had watched over her, protecting her in her world. But how? There was so much she didn't understand, but she did understand one thing: She had never really been alone.

"Hel … lo," said the woman approaching her, speaking slowly, as if unused to words and visitors.

Khia couldn't help but stare at the beautiful woman, with her bronze skin, amber eyes, and long sable hair that fell to her waist.

"A girl all alone, but not alone ... how strange ... it is to me," she smiled. "And yet you know my companions. Or is it ... perhaps ... that they know you?

"Not many visit me here in my kingdom. And fewer yet do I visit. I am ..." her voice trailed off, as if she were recollecting memories that she should never have lost. "Ah yes," and she laughed a sad laugh. "Things

must be moving at last. Things unbound." She stopped. "I am …
Timothea, and you … you are … Khia."

CHAPTER 15

The Pendant

In the cave, sitting with her legs crossed, Khia's eyes fluttered open.

"You have returned," said Nora.

Her limbs felt stiff and cold.

How long have I been away? Khia looked around the cave, not sure if she'd been gone for minutes, hours, or days.

Khia shivered. Awkwardly, she got to her feet; she stretched and rubbed her arms and legs trying to rid the stiffness that had settled into her joints.

Nora was pleased with how fast Khia had learned the first lesson, but the second lesson had taken much too long. Nora had expected that Khia would have been able to figure it out in a few minutes, not a few hours. She wondered what had gone wrong.

Nora knew that Khia was tired and most likely overwhelmed by her experiences, but she had one more lesson to teach her.

"What are you Khia? Do you know?" asked Nora harshly, pressing Khia for an answer, and not giving her any time to adjust to being back in the so-called real world.

Khia was cold; her body ached all over and she was tired. She'd been on her first dream-scape, or maybe it was a dream-walk. She didn't know what to call it and she really wanted to talk to Nora about what had happened to her, except then Nora had gone and thrown her a question like that. Khia shrugged her shoulders, not sure how to answer.

"You are a warrior," said Nora, giving her the answer.

"No I'm not," Khia reacted sharply.

"Do you know what a warrior is?" asked Nora patiently.

"Yeah, uh, someone who uses a sword," she said, thinking of Norbert.

"Yes, that can be partly true, but not entirely true," said Nora. Turning away, she walked to the ledge, looking intently at the large red orb setting and the abyss below; it was dusk and the night was fast approaching. Without warning, and with incredible speed, Nora turned and threw a sharp and lethal knife directly at Khia.

Oh my God, she wants to kill me!

And in that split second, Khia reacted.

Her heart quickened, adrenaline surged through her body, but conversely, the air around her felt thick and heavy. Her entire focus was on the steel blade coming towards her. It seemed to slow and then everything sped back up to normal time. Quicker than she would have thought possible, Khia bent her upper torso sideways, and the knife narrowly missed her. Turning, everything became reversed—the knife was moving away from her now, but still within reach. In a fluid motion, Khia extended her hand and gripped the hilt. She coiled her body back around, intently staring at Nora's heart, and ready to throw the knife.

Khia stopped.

What am I doing? Stunned, she brought her hand down and looked at the knife. It looked like a ceremonial knife—the hilt studded in turquoise and silver, the blade heavy and sharp—and could easily pierce flesh.

She had come so close to throwing it ... come so close to killing Nora, and what scared her the most was that she hadn't even blinked. It had all been so automatic ... so easy.

Nora laughed aloud. "A true warrior if ever I saw one."

With highly charged emotions—anger, fear, and disgust—Khia stared at Nora, and a second later, tossed the knife away, hearing it clatter and come to rest near the edge of the rock face. A few more inches and it would have toppled over the edge.

"Interesting, isn't it Khia," said Nora, pausing. "Your reaction betrays you. You have a true warrior's spirit and it comes from deep within you. But you must remember that a warrior's most powerful weapon is her intellect. You could have thrown the knife, but you chose differently."

Khia didn't respond.

"Not all fighters are true warriors," continued Nora.

Weren't all fighters warriors, and all warriors fighters? Khia listened, but couldn't quite grasp the nuances of Nora's words.

Nora stopped.

"Come," Nora extended her hand, "you have learned enough for one day. You're tired and we have a long trek home."

"But what about Timothea?" blurted out Khia.

"Timothea?" This time it was Nora who was taken aback.

"Was meeting Timothea not part of my lesson in the Dark World?" inquired Khia.

In that moment, a dry and subtle wind sprang up and a faint voice could be heard, manipulating the air around them in shadowed waves and patterns, "For you, Khia." A pendant materialized in the air by Khia. Without thinking, she opened her hand and it came to rest on her palm. It was a white bear's paw clutching a black stone. It was beautiful. "It was mine," the voice continued, "but meant for you."

Then, as gentle as a butterfly flapping its wings, the dark zephyr disappeared, and the air was still once more.

"A gift from Timothea," said Nora, in absolute wonderment. But what was even more surprising to Nora was that she'd seen one before ... just like this one.

The black stone within the bear claw twisted and turned, disappearing and reappearing playfully in the light. Protectively, Khia closed her palm around it.

†

Khia looked up at McBride, "I guess Nora's some kind of an Indian spirit woman."

"Something like that," he nodded.

"But what does that make you and Norbert?" asked Khia, looking curiously into his eyes.

McBride smiled, "That makes us friends."

†

Peering through her small-framed reading glasses, Nora sat in front of her computer, tapping away diligently on the keyboard. At her feet, the dogs contentedly slept. Sensing Norbert and McBride approach, Nora stopped and swiveled around to look at the two men.

"Now that you've spent some time with Khia, what do you think," asked Norbert.

"Khia is very strong," began Nora, "and she is much more than she appears."

They both nodded like proud parents.

"Khia had little problem getting into and out of the Dark World. She has shamanic talent. A true warrior. She even experimented with her new-found abilities, going back and forth between realms, honing her skills. She has many gifts. I'm rather pleased with how much she's learned."

"But there's more for her to learn. Some of it will be unpleasant and even painful," said Norbert.

McBride raised his concerns. "Does she have it in her?"

"Who can tell with these things, but yes ... I believe she has it in her," said Nora. "She has an affinity with steel that is quite astounding."

"But you're not telling us something," observed McBride.

"She's too young."

"Yeah, we know," said Norbert.

"You must do anything you can to postpone the inevitable," said Nora.

"Easier said that done," said McBride.

Norbert looked into Nora's eyes. "There's something else ... Spit it out woman."

"Something ..." Nora paused for a moment, "unexpected happened to Khia in the Dark World."

McBride motioned with his hand and Norbert nodded. They may have used different body language, but they were conveying the same message: Get on with it, Nora. Tell us what happened!

"Khia has met Timothea."

"And who is Timothea?" asked Norbert.

"Timothea is a myth, or at least ... I thought she was."

"A myth?" Norbert repeated.

"No kidding," said McBride, rather intrigued.

"The story of Timothea evolved into an Indian fairytale," said Nora. "Instead of telling our children the story of the big bad wolf, we told them the story of Timothea."

"I love the Brothers' Grimm fairytales. They make perfect bedtime stories," McBride laughed a little, trying to lighten up the mood.

He too had noticed that Nora was shaking, and watched as Norbert put his great arms about her.

Taking a slow deep breath, Nora continued. "I don't know where to begin. There are many different stories of her, mostly made up, or so I thought ... but now I believe that there is more than a grain of truth in the tales." She laughed, "As a small child, I spent a few wakeful nights, afraid Timothea would come for me and steal my totem animals."

Nora picked up a pen, looking at its sharp end, "The original stories can be traced back thousands of years," said Nora, steadying herself. "Timothea ... Timothea, you see, was the very first female shaman."

McBride, who loved stories, elbowed Norbert, who sat beside him, and whispered, "Ohhh, I can tell this is going to be a good one."

He was shushed by Norbert, who was just as enthralled.

And Nora began her tale ...

CHAPTER 16

The Fourth Apprentice

Full Circle

Long long ago, when the world was young, there were no female shamans, for it was forbidden.

Girls stayed with their mothers and sisters, gathering, mending, and caring for the young and the very old. Boys followed their fathers and became hunters and warriors. It was the men who protected the village, and it was the men who made war.

These were the traditional ways, the way things had always been ...

Until Timothea.

As a young girl, Timothea went to help the village shaman and his wife. The village shaman's wife was named Widowmaker, after the spider that kills with a single bite. She was a great healer and midwife, and she taught Timothea about plants and herbs—how they could be used to heal, how they could be used to bring relief from suffering ... and how they could be used to bring death.

Widowmaker and her husband were already old, perhaps ancient, by this time. Time was running short for them and the Shaman needed an apprentice, to whom he could pass on his knowledge. Sadly, they had never been blessed with children, but they had trust in the Universe and believed there was a reason for everything.

Now it so happened that the Chief of the tribe had been blessed with three sons, but unfortunately, he had not been blessed with clever sons. In fact, his three sons were best characterized as oafs. They were lazy, stupid, arrogant young men, who (because their father was the Chief) behaved as if they were entitled to anything and everything.

The Chief's three sons were named Standing Grass, Falling Leaves, and Angry Bear. Standing Grass moved so slowly that people said the grass grew in-between his steps, Falling Leaves was clumsy and people laughed at him because of how often he tripped over his own feet, but the worst of his three sons was Angry Bear. Angry Bear possessed formidable strength and a terrible temper.

The Chief grew distressed. He too was getting old and he worried about his people, for his sons, and about what would happen after his death. He struggled with the problem until one night the answer came to him in the form of a dream.

The following morning, he told his three sons of his pronouncement. All three, he had decided, would become the Shaman's new apprentices. He told them that, when they had finished their long tuition with the Shaman, one son would become the new leader of their people, one son would become the village shaman, and to motivate them further (or so he thought), the third would be given a choice between learning the skills of the village women or being shunned and driven from the village, to make his way alone in the world.

After months of patient teaching, the chief's sons (except perhaps for Angry Bear, whose motives were thought to be dubious) had barely grasped even the most rudimentary of magical skill. Widowmaker, however, had positioned Timothea close, so that on the day the Shaman lost his temper, he called Timothea to his side and asked her to follow his instructions. It was said by some that it was an act of desperation, others, a state of folly, while others yet believed that it was brilliant insight, and that Widowmaker had planned it all.

Needless to say, Timothea easily accomplished the series of tasks the Shaman set before her.

Amazed at the girl's skill, the Shaman decided then and there that she must be allowed to learn. There was no other way. He knew their time was growing thin and that, without Timothea, their knowledge would be lost ... forever.

Standing Grass and Falling Leaves accepted Timothea, but Angry Bear grew more hostile. Angry Bear complained bitterly; he said that it was an indecency ... an abomination that a girl should be privy to shamanic knowledge. The village shaman would not be swayed.

Angry Bear stormed away and confronted his father about the violation of their laws and demanded recourse. His father dismissed him, but Angry Bear would not be easily swayed and forced his father's hand, demanding a remedy for Timothea's trespass. A Great Meeting was called among their peoples.

For three days and three nights, impassioned pleas were debated and argued. In the end, it was decided that the risk of losing the old village shaman's knowledge was far too great. Timothea was allowed to be the fourth apprentice, and all of the Chief's peoples were sworn to abide by this ruling.

Except whispers were heard. Angry Bear began to gather a following, and his followers swore on their very souls and to the great spirits that they would one day return things to how they were meant to be. .

But such things take time to manifest. Not wanting to be bested by a girl, Timothea's presence caused a profound effect on the Chief's sons. The three brothers focused diligently on their teacher's teachings and this was even more true for Angry Bear; he had found the motivation to learn, but his anger towards her festered and he did everything in his power to make it difficult for her ... but she was not so easily swayed.

In time, Falling Leaves and Standing Grass became quite competent, but it was Timothea and Angry Bear who grew powerful ... almost, it can be said, as powerful as the old Shaman.

Nora paused.

The Spirit World did call to take the Chief, the Shaman, and Widowmaker. Widowmaker's dying words warned Timothea to be very, very careful, for she knew the perverse nature and depravity that Angry Bear held in his heart.

A Great Gathering was called to honor those who had died that year and to proclaim their new leaders. Angry Bear became the new chief and Falling Leaves and Timothea became the village shamans. It was said that Standing Grass chose to work with the women, but ridiculed by Angry Bear and the men of the village, he lasted only four seasons, and then chose to live in exile.

As Chief, Angry Bear feigned humility, but he soon revealed his true nature and found reason to ban Timothea from practicing shamanism. In secret, however, Timothea continued to practice her craft, desiring to learn more and to help her people. She heeded Widowmaker's warning; she was careful, but she was not careful enough. Angry Bear had spies everywhere and they accused her of practicing the dark forbidden arts ... and because of her violation, Timothea was sentenced to death.

"What? Hold on! What do you mean 'sentenced to death'?" asked McBride.

"Shush," Norbert interjected. "Let Nora finish her story."

Nora nodded slowly and continued.

Although imprisoned, Timothea escaped, slipping through Angry Bear's magic. Angry Bear vowed that he would find her, and destroy her. He and his secret coven of warriors pursued her relentlessly.

Not a lot is known about the secret coven, but what is known is that Angry Bear chose the strongest and fiercest warriors—those who desired knowledge of the dark arts. These warriors swore allegiance to him and to him alone. The few who passed the very difficult initiation trials were branded with a Red Bear tattoo on their forearm—a symbol of the highest order.

For a lifetime, Timothea wandered alone. Some said she lived in the wilderness, some said she settled in the northern lands, but according to our legends, Timothea collected the seeds of knowledge that had been scattered by the spirits when the world was created and thus became so powerful that she was able to build a bridge across to the spirit world, allowing her spirit animals to cross over into the world of the living.

Interestingly, there are many legends from other cultures that mention a powerful woman shaman, who visited and stayed sometimes for a few days, sometimes for many moons. In all of them, she is described as being very beautiful, and traveling with a silver wolf and a black bird.

Weary of exile and forever hiding from Angry Bear, Timothea created a world for herself—such was her great power. It was a paradise ... a land without evil, a world without strife, and a place where Angry Bear would never find her.

But Timothea grew lonely in her paradise. For what is paradise if you cannot share it with another?

Timothea sent out a call that reverberated throughout the magical mediums between the worlds—a cry that every shaman, wizard, and magi heard.

It was a challenge and a promise: The one to pass her tests would be granted immortality and share her world with her. Many answered her call, but the trials grew exponentially more difficult, weaning the weak, the inferior, and the foolish.

One man, however, caught Timothea's attention. Covered in metal that had once shone silver and gold, he rode on a swift and powerful charger. He had traveled great distances, fought many battles, and bested dragons and many horrific creatures.

The Knight overcame each and every obstacle set before him. Timothea watched as he stood before her last test: a wall of fire, which only one who was pure of heart could safely walk through unscathed.

The Knight walked through the wall of flames. But the moment he walked through, Timothea knew that while his heart was pure ... he loved another.

In an uncontrollable rage, Timothea locked him in a cold dungeon, like Angry Bear had done to her many years before.

However, other things were in play. Because Timothea had sent out a call through magical mediums—Angry Bear had tracked her down. Past primed for vengeance, he unleashed his unholy army of warriors and bound spirits upon her, broke her defenses, and entered her world.

The battle was fierce. If not for the brave knight, Timothea's world would have fallen.

He fought valiantly, until a red arrow pierced his armor. At that moment, Timothea learned the true and terrifying strength she possessed. Unrequited love, anger, and grief ... all filled her soul for this man, her Knight ... whose heart belonged to another, who had walked fearlessly through fire, and risked his life to defend her and her world.

In a cold fury, Timothea laid waste to Angry Bear's army of warriors, shamans, and spirits. In a final cataclysmic clash, she struck Angry Bear with a power so fierce that he could not stand against it; he was no match for the hurricane she unleashed upon him.

His army, it was said by some, was obliterated ... other say it was decimated. Needless to say, Angry Bear fled and he and his army of warriors, shamans, and spirits were never seen again. But many believe that he and his secret coven of Red Bear followers went into hiding to await their day of resurrection.

Standing Grass returned to his village and became the Chief. After the seasons he had spent with the village women and his years in exile, ostracized from his peoples, he had learned many things. As Chief, he led his people with wisdom and fairness until the end of his days.

Falling Leaves, the village shaman, turned out to be an excellent teacher and passed on his knowledge to many generations to follow.

"But what about Timothea?" asked McBride.

Nora smiled sadly.

After the battle, the Knight lay dying from a poisoned arrow that had pierced his heart. Timothea gathered the last vestiges of her power. Holding him in her arms, she healed his fatal wound, some saying that she literally pulled him from beyond the door of death itself ...

And it is on the day that the Knight left to continue his quest that Timothea's realm began to fade. Some say it was because her powers had been spent, others say it was because her heart had broken. Nevertheless, her beautiful world wilted and began to darken on the day he rode away.

"Cool story, Nora," said Norbert, his eyes glistening while McBride (not too discretely) wiped tears from his eyes.

"Wow! So Khia's met Timothea," said McBride, with pride in his voice.

Nora nodded, "Only one other person I know of has ever claimed to have seen and spoken to Timothea," said Nora.

"And who would that be?" asked Norbert.

"My father," answered Nora quietly.

"Rainbow Walker!" exclaimed Norbert.

"All these years," said Nora sadly, "and I never realized that he was speaking the truth."

McBride remained unusually silent.

"It's time you tell me everything you know," said Nora. "We've got to start connecting the pieces."

"That's not easy to explain," said Norbert.

"Try," Nora said firmly, her eyes narrowing.

"Don't give me that look," said Norbert.

"It was a straightforward assignment," McBride jumped in.

"We were instructed to deliver Khia and Devon to their grandmother's," said Norbert. "The challenge was too good to refuse, eh McBride?"

McBride shrugged his shoulders.

"All expenses paid, free travel, and a large bonus."

"And you know how much we love to travel," added McBride.

"So you were commissioned to take Khia and Devon to their grandmother's, in New York City, and that's all you know?" summarized Nora, trying to keep them on track.

Norbert nodded.

"Norbert!" she said.

"Okay, okay … it's a Portal in New York City."

"A Portal?"

"You sound surprised," said Norbert.

"I am," she replied.

"But … but you're a shaman," said Norbert.

"I travel through different realms in other ways." Nora smiled at McBride. "Just as well I'm sitting. It's a shock to learn that Timothea is real *and* that Portals really do exist!" Nora spoke slowly, taking it all in. She shook her head a little, in disbelief. "And what do you know about their grandmother?"

"Huh?"

"You didn't think it wise to ask?"

"Well ..." Norbert cleared his throat.

Nora frowned.

"I have a few theories of my own," interjected McBride.

"You do?" Norbert turned to his friend.

"We believe Khia and Devon are Lady Tiamore's grandchildren," said McBride.

"Lady Tiamore," Nora said. "How interesting. This just gets better and better."

"It does?" asks Norbert.

"It does!" said McBride, using the same words but meaning something totally different.

"Have you heard of her, Nora?" asked McBride.

"Yeah, I've heard of her." She paused. "Have you not listened to the story I've just told?" Nora smiled, "Timothea and the Knight? Well, the Knight's true love is Lady Tiamore."

"Small worlds," commented McBride.

"Wow," said Norbert. "So what was his quest?"

"I think we might have just figured that out too," said Nora.

CHAPTER 17

Down Stream

And oh, the river runs swifter now;
The eddies circle above my bow.
Swirl, swirl!
How the ripples curl?
In many a dangerous pool awhirl!
— Pauline Johnson 1861-1913. The Song My Paddle Sings

Some days later

Nora looked out the window of her cabin and watched Khia and Devon playing. "To have no cares in the world," she said to McBride, as she watched them stacking leaves in a pile and scattering them to the wind.

McBride nodded.

"It's one of the few times I've seen her laugh," commented Nora.

"Yeah, she's a serious little thing," said McBride, about to call them in to resume their studies.

Nora held his arm and said, "No. Let them play."

†

Summer holidays were over.

Unable to go to school, Khia and Devon spent their days in home study. Serious about education, McBride and Nora taught them many things beyond the school curriculum, but Khia needed to learn to fight, and for that, she needed Norbert. She wanted to ask him, and had come close a few times, but couldn't quite muster the courage.

Oddly enough, Norbert too was keen to teach Khia but wasn't sure how to broach the topic with his young charge. As it turned out, when the moment arrived, it was effortless.

Every morning at sunrise, Norbert took his great sword and went outside to greet the day. He drew it from its scabbard; it shone breathtakingly in the first light of dawn's new day. Norbert would begin his rare *Katas*, taught to him by great masters—men, and a few extraordinary women, dedicated to martial arts. Meticulously, he would go through long sequences that he had long ago honed and perfected, and were ingrained seamlessly within him.

Absorbed in movements that were executed with blurring speed and precision, he soon became aware of eyes observing him from the shadows.

Only a few minutes before, Khia had been sleeping when something in her dreams awakened her. Norbert's steel had called, and like a gentle breeze, asked her if this was the day that they should meet.

Khia stepped outside; the screen door slipped away from her fingers and banged shut. Unblinkingly, she watched the blur of light that flew around Norbert. She was mesmerized by his sword. Anyone who has experienced love at first sight might have an inkling of what Khia felt in that magical moment.

Khia wasn't sure how long she stood on the porch, enthralled by the blade and spellbound by the skill of its master.

Easing up, Norbert arrived at a cessation in his actions. He bowed to the young girl, acknowledging her presence. "Good morning," he said.

Norbert carefully laid his glistening weapon on the wooden table near him.

Khia, as if in a waking trance, walked towards his sword.

Norbert stopped her with his outstretched hand. "Khia," he said in a serious tone that startled her from her reverie. "My sword is unique; it is a blade that has awareness ... a life of its own."

"Yes," she replied, in a bit of a daze, "it called to me."

Stepping aside, Norbert gave his consent for her to proceed, to introduce herself to the sword.

Khia held her breath and cautiously approached the sword, noticing an intricately carved tree on its hilt.

She looked up at him, asking him silently what it meant.

"It is the tree of life," replied Norbert.

"It's very old," Khia said.

"Yes, it was forged a very long time ago."

As her fingers traced the hilt, silvery blue sparks jumped across the span. Unsure, Khia paused and looked up at Norbert.

Norbert nodded encouragingly.

Her gaze returned to the weapon, and she wrapped both her hands around its hilt. Everything around her grew quiet, a hush ...

There were no sounds in the wilderness, no breeze to rustle the leaves on the trees. Norbert himself seemed to fade into the background and it was as if there were only two things that were real: her and the sword.

The moment of contact was unlike anything she had ever experienced before. A thrilling euphoric gasp went through her and she could not suppress the rising elation within her. She had expected it to be heavy, but it was light—the perfect weight for her. She felt the hilt as it changed in her hand. What had been made for Norbert's large hands, in moments, fit her hands perfectly ... like molded clay.

In a surprisingly graceful arc, Khia lifted the weapon from the table. She felt herself become centered and calm.

"Khia," spoke Norbert, "the blade has bonded with you and will never hurt you."

Khia looked up at Norbert and smiled.

"Throw the weapon into the air," he commanded.

Khia hesitated. She didn't want to let it go ... not this soon.

"I have set this blade free many times. It always returns to me," he explained.

She obeyed and threw the sword as high as she could into the air, and in a bright flash, the blade turned into liquid and formed into two swords—identical except that one was smaller than the other. Norbert caught both effortlessly.

"Today, you have been accepted as a Student of the Sword. Would you like to spar with me?"

"Yes," Khia whispered hoarsely.

From the moment Khia had thrown the sword into the air, Norbert had seen an ability and naturalness within Khia that he hadn't seen before, and saw that she was a true warrior, albeit untrained, just as Nora had said.

The sound that awakened the household was of steel ringing on steel, as Khia and Norbert embarked on the ancient art form.

McBride and Nora watched from the kitchen window.

Devon ran out to watch, wide-eyed, and desperately wishing that it could have been him holding the sword and sparing with Uncle Norbert.

To Devon's great disappointment, Nora escorted him back into the house, but as the young boy was led away, he too heard the softest whispered promise that he had not been forgotten … and that, one day, he too would be called.

†

A chaotic swirl of pixels coalesced into the image of Ms Percival. She looked decidedly distressed as she was escorted into a government building, its lobby jammed beyond its capacity with photographers jostling, lights flashing, and reporters yelling out a stream of unanswered questions.

"Nora, can you play the clip again?" asked Norbert.

Norbert's attention was drawn to someone in the crowd. It could have been anyone, but he knew who it was: a colleague of sorts, someone he had had the misfortune of running into on more than one occasion. The quality of the image was out of focus and blurred, but Norbert was sure it was one of the brothers.

Norbert stroked his scarred cheek.

"This is not good," said Norbert, looking at McBride. "We're going to have to leave sooner than I thought. We have to get them through the … get them to their grandmother's."

Before McBride could utter a word, Norbert held up his hand to McBride and turned to Nora. "Nora, what do you think?"

Nora didn't answer and instead reached over to a colorful tarot deck. She shuffled the deck and a card practically exploded from the deck, flitted to the ground, and landed face up.

The Death card.

Norbert looked at her questioningly.

"You have your ways to divine and I have mine," she closed her eyes as if she were listening. "People are usually frightened of the Death card, but it is not always death. Change for many is a kind of a death. Death is coming, death stalks." After a long pause, she said, "It will be risky, but Khia has to see my father."

"You can talk now, McBride," said Norbert.

"Well thank you, Norbert," replied McBride. "Maybe we should have gone straight to New York."

"You're not helping, McBride," responded Norbert.

"Nora's right. Rainbow Walker may be able to help," said McBride, in all seriousness.

Norbert got up and looked out the window, looked back at Nora and then at McBride, and then looked out the window again. "Why'd I even ask?" he shook his head. "Let's do it."

"You're going to need more firepower," said Nora. "A sword and an Uzi are nice things, but it's not going to be enough to protect you. McBride, do you remember my cousin Sheila?"

McBride nodded, remembering. "Oh yeah. Do I ever!"

"You can meet up with her while Khia and I see my father. She can provide you with an assortment of ..." Nora smiled, "unique hardware, so to speak."

"Why do I have a bad feeling about this," muttered Norbert.

"You know, Norbert, you should try being more positive," said McBride.

†

Ms Percival exited out of the back door. She wanted to avoid all the reporters and journalists that were staked out at the front door. It was dark and well past midnight. As she walked towards her car in the darkened parking lot, she heard a noise behind her.

She quickened her pace.

Twenty feet away, three figures stepped out from underneath a lamp post, blocking her advance.

She stopped.

"Hello, Ms Percival."

She recognized the voice, and turned. In one hand was a revolver, and in the other was a sword that she called her own.

"Oh I don't think that will be necessary. Do you?" Burdock asked, with his own sword in his hand. "We just want to talk," and he laughed.

†

Early next morning, well before sunrise, they drove the two-toned blue truck about a mile east, over rough terrain, to the river. They got into an old aluminum boat with an overly powerful engine; the weight of it forced them to sit towards the front of the boat in order to balance it … otherwise its bow hovered high above the water.

With a sharp pull of the starter cord, the engine purred to life and McBride piloted them down river.

For Khia, it was an amazing trip through the wilderness, especially when they saw a couple of black bears, and a moose munching on weeds in a marshy area.

They followed the contours of the sacred but scarred landscape. Khia could feel the beauty, strength, and power of this place: of air, water, and land. At times, suspended on the river, Khia felt slightly disorientated, unable to discern which way was up and which way was down, as a perfect reflection of the sky was mirrored in the water. It was as if they were somewhere in between Heaven and Earth.

Near the final stage of their journey, they came to a very large lake. For miles, because of the choppy water, they hugged the coastline. Leaving the safety of Nora's protective forest, they moved towards the trappings of civilization: railway tracks, roads, and bridges. They reached their destination, which was a comparatively large city for the north—a community of about eighty thousand.

Wasting no time, they split up, leaving the boat unattended. Nora and Khia went east, to the nursing home where Nora's father was a resident, and Norbert, McBride, and Devon went to the center of town to meet Nora's cousin Sheila.

Khia and Nora arrived at the gates of a nine-story, red-brick building. Going up to the main desk, Nora signed in. She didn't have to read the resident's rules about the visitation hours being between nine in the morning and nine at night, and no pets allowed except for approved therapy dogs.

Nora and Khia took the elevator and went up to the sixth floor, heading towards room 616B.

"Hello Nora," an elderly resident called out as they walked down the hallway.

Nora waved in greeting but didn't stop as was her usual habit.

Khia didn't know what to expect. What was a great Shaman supposed to look like? Nora had said that her father was old but stepping into the semiprivate room had in no way prepared her. It was a shock. One occupant, an emaciated old man, lay unresponsive in one of the beds, surrounded by a host of tubes and wires. In the other bed, an old but spry Indian man sat up. He had a friendly manner and a charming smile. He was attended to by two nurses, who seemed to have their hands full as he openly flirted with them.

"Shouldn't you act your age, old man, and let your nurses get on with their jobs?" stated Nora with a sly smile.

"Nora," answered the man, delighted to see her. "Shit, these days I'm more like Lying Flat Grey Arse—Oops," he said, seemingly noticing Khia for the first time, "sorry for the profanity."

Nora laughed, "Grey Horse, meet Khia ... and I'm sure she's heard worse."

Khia smiled.

"Have you come to free me from this hideaway of perversion and relentless care?"

"Not me, you old trifler. What would your nurses do without you?" Nora countered.

He laughed warm-heartedly.

"How's Dad," Nora asked in a more serious voice.

Grey Horse looked at the other bed. "Not well," he answered truthfully, empathy showing in his deep voice and magnetic eyes.

Khia was stunned. She had thought Nora's father was the robust elder, Grey Horse. It was the other man, the non-responsive old Indian, who was Nora's father.

"I'll leave you with him," said Grey Horse. With little help from the nurses, he got out of bed and into his wheelchair.

Khia saw that the man had only one leg. "Diabetes kid," he said, looking at Khia. "When you get up there in age, it gets harder and harder to control. Until I get my new leg, and considering the alternative, one leg will do me just fine." He winked playfully at her as he wheeled himself out of the room.

CHAPTER 18

Grandfather's Song

"This is my father, Rainbow Walker," said Nora, motioning Khia towards the frail body.

Hovering between two worlds, Rainbow Walker was nearing the end of his life. His breathing was shallow and he showed no awareness of the world around him.

The sounds and smells disturbed Khia: strong sanitized hospital smells and the rancid odors of the dying.

"Khia," Nora's voice cracked with emotion, "I have to talk with the nurses. They want to move him to the seventh floor. Can you stay here? I'll be right back."

Khia didn't want to be left alone but nodded. As soon as Nora left the room, Khia moved as far away from the bed as she could. Nervously, her hand played with the pendant that hung around her neck on a leather strap. The black stone suddenly spun around of its own volition, twisted, and twirled out of the clutches of the bear's claw, skittering onto the floor and under Rainbow Walker's bed, out of sight.

"Oh, no!" gasped Khia.

Under Rainbow Walker's bed, Khia was using her hands like a blind person, searching the cold floor for the black stone, when she heard a man's voice.

From her vantage point, she saw that someone was in the room, silently walking towards the bed.

A moment later, he poked his head under the bed. "Nice view isn't it?" he spoke humorously.

A good-looking Indian man, who appeared to be in his late forties, with deep laugh lines around his almond-shaped eyes, looked at her kindly, "You're the girl who came in with Nora."

Khia nodded.

"Did you lose something?" he asked her.

Khia, visibly upset, did not know what to say.

"Let me help you," he offered. "So what are we looking for?" he asked, getting down onto the floor.

How could she explain that it was part of a pendant she'd gotten from another world—Timothea's world?

"Is it bigger than a breadbox or is it the size of a pea? Or perhaps it is this little black seed."

How could I have missed it? thought Khia. *It was right in front of my eyes.*

The stone glowed with an energy that had not been there before.

The two of them crawled out from under the bed.

"Interesting little thing isn't it?" Like a magician, he made the stone disappear and reappear. He brought his hand just in front of her and there it was in his hand again. "Life starts from a small seed," he said, as he reached out, gently lifted the pendant, placed the black stone back where it belonged in the White Bear Claw, and then released it to hang once again from its leather strap.

"Thank you," she said. "My name is Khia. Do you know Nora?"

"Ah, I've known her since she was a baby," he answered, although he looked younger than Nora.

†

"Sorry it took me so long," said Nora, as she entered the room some time later. A large cache of documents and papers were in her arms.

Khia turned to introduce her new friend, but he was gone. Khia was going to say something about the man, but Nora looked upset.

"How is your father?" asked Khia.

Nora looked at her father's tortured body, with tears in her eyes, and said. "He's not ready to die. He has more to do in this world."

"That's what the man in the room said to me," answered Khia surprised.

"What man?" Nora asked.

But Khia realized that she didn't know his name.

"He was—" Before Khia could say anything more, they were interrupted by an unexpected stirring from Rainbow Walker's bed.

Painfully, the old man's head turned, neck bones cracking from lack of use, and his eyes unfocused. They heard a shallow, unintelligible, raspy voice that issued from his dry, thin, cracked lips. The second time he said it, they understood. "Run."

Nora and Khia looked at each other, horror written on their faces.

In a mad dash, they ran from the room.

"Not the elevator," cried Nora. "The stairs!"

I've made a terrible mistake! Nora's thoughts shouted. *I should never have brought Khia here! Instead of protecting her and keeping her safe, I have brought her into harm's way!*

CHAPTER 19

White World Malls

Sticking with McBride's philosophy (*Why walk when you can drive?*), Norbert, McBride, and Devon thumbed a lift and headed into town in the back of an old beat-up pickup truck. Wearing flannel shirts, jeans, and hunting hats, they blended fairly well with the members of the northern community.

Arriving five minutes early, they roamed the mall waiting for Nora's cousin Sheila. Their rendezvous point was a large box store that carried just about everything at a discount. It was a place that was almost heaven to McBride, and mostly hell to Norbert.

"Nice winter styles this year," McBride commented. "Prices are a little steep. You know, in China I could buy three times the amount for what they're asking here ..." McBride droned on.

Norbert hated shopping and he couldn't care less about prices. His ideal shopping experience was seeing, buying, and (the best part) leaving.

Bored beyond comprehension, Norbert felt uneasy and exposed waiting for Cousin Sheila, who seemed to be taking her sweet time. "Must be Indian time," grumbled Norbert.

"I'll wait for Sheila. Why don't you take Devon to the toy section," suggested McBride.

Norbert nodded. "Sure, the kid must be bored."

In the toy department, Devon was in paradise. Colorful buttons to push, cranks to twist, and balls to bounce. Happy to be surrounded by such treasures, it never occurred to Devon that, if he had asked, Norbert would have bought him just about anything.

Devon, with a military toy jet in his hand and his own ample imagination, ran up and down the aisles, pretending to be flying at supersonic speed—seven times faster than the speed of sound. With some pretty convincing sound effects, and his eyes squinted slightly shut to create a realistic effect, he was absorbed in his make-believe world.

†

Norbert watched as the small boy disappeared down one aisle and reappeared up another.

"Devon," Norbert called out, exasperated, but Devon ran from the toy section totally immersed in play.

Catching a glimpse of the young boy flying his jet in and out of the racks of woman's clothing, Norbert went after him. *Strange*, thought Norbert. The closer he got, the quicker and more elusive the boy became.

"Kids," muttered Norbert. He never did understand them.

†

In the toy section, Devon stopped.

Where was Uncle Norbert? He'd been right here only a moment ago. He carefully placed his toy jet on a rack.

"Uncle Norbert?" he called anxiously, as he attempted to retrace his steps. Although he tried to be brave, it wasn't long before tears welled in his eyes as he imagined all kinds of horrible things.

A teenage girl, who was one of the store's employees, dressed in red and white, not only heard him calling for Norbert but saw his distress.

"Hello, I'm Sandra S," she said, as she approached Devon and showed him her plastic name tag. "Are you lost?"

Devon nodded.

It was easy for a kid to get lost in the large and disorientating aisles; it happened all the time. She bent down to Devon's level and offered to help.

The two, hand-in-hand, went looking for Norbert just as a beautiful tanned woman, with black eyes and dressed in red, appeared out of nowhere. She threw her arms around Devon and hugged him closely.

"Devon, where have you been?" the woman cooed; Devon felt a sharp pinprick in his left arm. He felt light-headed and very strange and wobbly-like.

"I've been looking all over for you. You know you're not supposed to wander off, you naughty, naughty boy," she reprimanded him in such a way that she sounded just like a distraught mother, cross and relieved at the same time—thankful that nothing had happened to her precious, precious child.

"Thank you, Sandra," said the woman. She turned and whisked the small boy away.

Devon looked at Sandra as he was being pulled away; he tried to call out but couldn't.

Watching them leave, Sandra sensed that something was wrong. *Kid's probably just embarrassed!* Sandra rationalized the situation, and then noticed that her name tag had flipped over. *Strange*, she thought, righting it … but when she saw her manager, she quickly got back to stacking the shelves and pushed the incident to the back of her mind.

Teetering on his feet, Devon was unable to escape the woman's iron grip.

"You and your sister Khia have caused us enough problems," hissed the woman, in a voice that had lost any pretense of its warmth now that no one was around to hear.

Devon was roughly dragged down more aisles to the back of the store, which was jammed packed with tall racks full of merchandise; they were making a beeline towards a metal door with bold black uppercase letters: EMERGENCY EXIT.

With just his eyes, Devon looked desperately for McBride and Norbert.

All of a sudden, the world around Devon exploded. Merchandise crashed to the floor and he fell to the ground. Devon watched as a great hulking figure tackled the woman. She was thrown backwards and heavy boxes tumbled on top of her and her attacker.

Norbert emerged from the great heap like a mad mucker, all muscles, eyes, and teeth. Devon felt himself firmly grabbed about the waist, and like a sack of potatoes, slung over a large shoulder.

"Come on kid, it's time we leave this place. The service is lousy." Under his breath, he muttered to himself, "How'd they get onto us so fast?"

The mere presence of Norbert filled Devon with complete confidence, but when he looked over Norbert's shoulder and saw the dazed figure rise feebly from the wreckage, he startled. The figure that emerged wasn't that of the woman in red but of a mean-looking Indian man, with a red bear tattoo on his arm and murderous black eyes that were angrily staring at him. It was an image that would haunt him in nightmares for years to come.

"We gotta get out of this maze," said Norbert.

With long gliding strides, they moved towards the front of the store.

"Ohhh shit!" Norbert swore under his breath.

Ahead of them, three police officers blocked the entrance. *That was too quick,* Norbert thought, but he soon realized that they were simply conversing with the attractive teller, oblivious to anything having happened in the store.

"Kid," whispered Norbert to his young charge, "we're going to walk right out of here as if it were the most natural thing in the world. Do you think you can do that?"

Devon nodded, although he was still a little unsteady on his feet.

A clamor of noise erupted and the chaos expanded exponentially around them. The sound of gun shots caused the police officers to look directly at Norbert, as if he were the one responsible for the mayhem.

Norbert grabbed Devon and dove for cover.

"Damn," swore Norbert. "I mean darn," he corrected, realizing his poor choice of language in front of the young boy.

The police officers crouched behind the tills, and shoppers started screaming and running for the exits.

"Heads up," came a friendly voice. Norbert deftly caught the high-powered rifle and two boxes of ammunition that McBride threw his way.

McBride rolled towards them with a smile on his face. "Sheila came through." He patted two large rucksacks full of hardware.

"Who are the trigger-happy jokers behind us?" asked Norbert, loading his rifle and detecting the group of figures closing in.

"Cowboys and Indians," answered McBride, shrugging his shoulders.

"Are the brothers involved in this?" asked Norbert.

"Must be," he said, checking his sights.

"Funny how they show up at the most inopportune times," said McBride sarcastically, as he fired a shot towards the back of the store.

Hearing a grunt, McBride commented, "Someone's got something to think about wouldn't you say?"

"Sure thing," replied Norbert.

"Good thing it's hunting season eh, Norbert? You think they'll have a blow-out sale because of our little visit?"

"How can you still be thinking of shopping at a time like this?"

"I'm a true shopper at heart," answered McBride. "Always loved haggling. You know in Egypt ... ahh, I loved Cairo ... such a—"

"Time and place, McBride," said Norbert, as he winked at Devon. "I think it's time we blow this place."

"Literally or figuratively?" asked McBride.

"A little of both, I'd imagine," replied Norbert.

"How about we go for a fifty-percent sale? Or better yet, a fire sale?"

Norbert nodded and issued instructions. "We move forward and cut through the line of cops. It'll be easier than turning back."

"The squeeze play, got it," agreed McBride.

"Are you ready, Devon?" asked Norbert.

Devon nodded.

"Okay, little buddy, let's go."

Devon was well protected by the two men as they moved like a well-rehearsed team. With well-placed shots, security cameras were disabled, the sprinkler system was engaged, and the alarm system went off.

In a flash, the three desperadoes moved laterally and were up and over the checkout counter. One well-placed bullet and the glass shattered as they sprinted through the sliding glass doors. A repeated recorded message thanked them for shopping at Wally's World and to please come again.

"Hey, hear that, we're welcomed back," laughed McBride, as he turned around and laid a barrage of bullets aimed at the cowboys, purposefully missing an inexperienced police officer, and showering him in an explosion of glass, wood, and melamine.

"I think you scared him, McBride."

"Uh, he'll laugh about it one day when he's older."

Norbert and McBride promptly commandeered a police vehicle. With a long squeal of tires, burning rubber, and white smoke that filled the parking lot, they made their escape. Weaving in, out, and over medians, McBride avoided the traffic that was backed up in both directions.

Siren blazing, they peeled through red lights and headed towards the lake.

The three police officers, a little more than shell shocked, tried a half-hearted attempt to pursue the culprits, but as they came upon their vehicles, knew they weren't going anywhere, hindered by oil slicked on asphalt, slashed tires, and failed engines.

No one noticed the middle-aged Indian woman calmly walking away. Sheila smiled, pleased that she had done her part to facilitate Norbert and McBride's escape. A moment later, however, she frowned when she spotted a group of men, and an Indian—who prominently displayed the symbol of the Red Bear Cult on his forearm. She watched in horror as they got into a revving, supercharged black truck, and squealed out of the parking lot.

†

Nora and Khia ran as fast as they could to the wharf and jumped in the boat. Khia threw off their lines and Nora gunned the engine.

High on the bow, Khia scanned the coastline for her brother, Norbert, and McBride.

Nora looked at the fuel gage, concerned.

Sensing they were in trouble, Nora called out into the wind, "Norbert, McBride, Devon ... Where are you?"

CHAPTER 20

Bridges, Boats and Trains

In the stolen patrol car, Norbert turned on the police radio. It crackled with shouting staccato voices: W*hat the hell ... going on ... are the suspects ... police car... south ...*

Topping the hill, Norbert yelled, "No way. They can't be this good!"

A thousand feet before them, blocking any further progress, were eight black trucks filled with muscled mercenaries and tough-looking Indians with their large guns trained on them.

"Have we become that predictable?" asked McBride.

They both looked at each other, and in unison, said, "Nah."

"Jinx," laughed Devon, unaware of the danger they were in.

"Someone's really really clever at guessing our next move," muttered McBride.

"This is a most unfortunate development."

In a long skid, laying down a thick layer of black rubber and leaving dark gray smoke behind them, McBride turned the vehicle around and sped away, initiating a high speed chase.

"We have to get to the lake!" yelled Norbert.

"The dirt road," Norbert pointed.

"That's not a dirt road; that's a goat path," McBride retorted, but swerved onto it anyway. Bouncing, skidding, and dodging around and over boulders and branches, McBride steered them as far as he could before the vehicle was irredeemably stuck, twenty yards short of the rocky escarpment.

They positioned themselves behind the police vehicle.

"What do we have?" asked Norbert, referring to Sheila's hardware supply.

"A couple of hundred rounds and two full rucksacks, one for me, and one for you," smiled McBride.

"That'll do," replied Norbert.

"What do you think is in the trunk?" asked McBride curiously.

"Don't wait for my permission."

McBride opened the trunk and found a treasure trove. "Oh yeah!" he exclaimed with enthusiasm. "Cop cars have such an interesting assortment of stuff."

The posse, in their four-wheel-drive vehicles, approached in a single line, the dust signaling their imminent arrival.

Ruffling Devon's hair, Norbert said, "You're cool kid," and made sure he stayed hidden behind the car.

Devon looked up at him with wide eyes that were filled with trust.

McBride whispered to Norbert, "Do you think they got Nora and the little kid's sister?"

"No," Devon answered, pointing to the open water.

"Sharp eyes, kid," said McBride.

Barely visible was a small aluminum boat, its bow unnaturally high on the water, patrolling the coast.

"Yup, I'd recognize that craft anywhere," responded Norbert. "I think it's time for us to go on the offensive, wouldn't you say?"

"Couldn't agree with you more. Time these guys learn who they're dealing with. We're not just ordinary hacks; we invented the term."

Deafening sounds of explosions, windscreens shattering, and tires exploding caused the approaching posse to jump for cover, taking away their quaint idea that this was going to be a Sunday jaunt.

Rule Number One: Never underestimate Norbert and McBride—especially when they go on the offensive!

"How are we going to attract Nora's attention," shouted Norbert, pulling the trigger on a really big gun that he aimed at one of the SUVs.

"Leave that to me," answered McBride with a smile. And with a sharp pull of a trigger, a canister flew through the air. Purple smoke spewed out and filled the area.

"Smoke signals, McBride! Smart thinking."

"Seems fitting under the circumstances, being in Indian country and all," grinned McBride.

"Khia sees us," said Devon triumphantly, jumping up and down and waving to his sister.

"Good job kid, but keep your head down," commanded Norbert, dragging the kid down to where it was safer.

Norbert grinned. A plan formed inside his mind as two opportunities presented themselves: the boat to the south and a bridge to the east. And when Norbert heard a mournful sound not that far away on the horizon, he smiled broadly, recounting his options. "Three."

"Devon, McBride, we have a bridge to cross."

"We gotta find a way to tell Nora to meet us there," said McBride.

"She'll know," said Norbert.

"Think we can do it?" asked McBride.

"Why do you ask stupid questions, McBride?" said Norbert. Retaliating with two well-placed shots, they made a run for it.

†

Khia spotted the smoke. She pointed and crawled even higher onto the bow. She hung on as she felt the craft turn.

Their tiny boat, on the large deep lake, neared the bridge, spanning a rock gorge that was a couple of hundred feet wide.

Khia and Nora scanned the escarpment. Hope renewed when they saw them. Fear returned when they saw the number of men fanning out behind them.

Nora, struggling with the boat against the strong current, said, "We're not in position yet."

Up ahead, Khia looked at the bridge, which was at least seventy feet above the water. Wide-eyed, she said, "No, no ... They can't possibly be thinking of that!"

†

Norbert and McBride always kept a few tricks up their sleeves.

Running and avoiding bullets, tracers, and blasts, Norbert and McBride shielded Devon with their bodies.

Everyone heard the violent, unapologetic cry of the Northern Express, one hundred and thirty-seven cars full of coal, timber, and iron ore, barreling down the track and heading east; it was late and had no intentions of stopping for anything.

The commander looked through his binoculars and realized, a little too late, what was going down. He yelled out his orders into his microphone, "Kill them now you idiots. All of them!"

"Clarification on the order, sir," a questioning voice came over the line. "There's a kid."

Sharpshooters moved in.

"Damn," swore Devon, as bullets rang about them. "Oh, I mean darn," he copied Norbert's words verbatim.

"You're a bad influence on the kid," McBride accused Norbert.

"Me?" said Norbert, feigning innocence.

With the train, chugging towards them, Norbert said, "Wait. Wait. Wait." And then yelled, "Now!"

The second they dashed onto the bridge, McBride pulled the trigger on the last canister and they were shrouded in thick smoke. In a fluid motion, he threw it and picked up Devon.

Devon had never been so close to a train before. It was the loudest thing he had ever heard in his life. The entire bridge shook. But he wasn't scared.

Across the narrow ties they ran, barely a foot from the squealing steel wheels and inches from a seventy foot drop into the cold water below. Midway across, they held their position, waiting for Nora to get a little closer to the bridge. Bullets ricocheted around them, but the train acted like a massive moving shield of protection.

Just as the last of the freight cars passed, Norbert yelled, "Jump!"

McBride threw his arsenal over, tightening his grip on Devon, and jumped.

Khia screamed as she watched McBride and Devon falling through the air and crash into the cold water.

The shock of the frigid water was electric, but a moment later, Devon felt himself propelled up and out of the water and into the boat … and into the arms of his sister.

Khia threw a blanket over him and ordered him to stay down.

Teeth chattering, Devon nodded, knowing that when he grew up he wanted to be just like Norbert and McBride.

McBride torpedoed out of the water into the center of the boat. He rolled, caught a loaded rifle that Nora tossed his way, and fired a number of shots that were timed perfectly, just as Norbert launched himself off the bridge.

In the air, Norbert twisted and turned, firing off a couple of rounds before he too plunged into the frigid water.

Khia watched as a hand emerged from the water, gripping the side of the boat.

Nora gunned the powerful engine. Dragged by the boat, Norbert (seemingly oblivious to the cold and buffeting waves) kept shooting until he was out of range.

With a powerful heave, Norbert pulled himself onto the speeding boat.

Camouflaged mercenaries and disbelieving Indians swarmed the bridge. Too late!

†

At the edge of the cliff, staring dispassionately down at the fleeing aluminum boat, stood Cocklebur and four men: the mercenary commander with a rifle slung over his shoulder, two Indians with red bear tattoos on their forearms, and Mr. Elliot holding his briefcase.

"One little, two little, three little Indians," spoke Cocklebur, his cold eyes narrow with contempt. "It seems we have too many Chiefs and not enough Indians." His eyes glared at Mr. Elliot. "She will not be pleased."

Mr. Elliot gripped his briefcase even tighter, his knuckles noticeably white.

"Red," Cocklebur called out to the Indian.

The Indian nodded. He looked at his blood brother (the other Indian with the same red bear tattoo on his forearm) who stood at his side. They bowed their heads and they began to chant.

"Niinii ha biidsatood dkaanmak."

"Vidkaaba, mji-giizh wed aakwaa; aakwaadendaa." Their eerie voices, full of energy and power, carried on the wind.

And then they raised their staffs.

"Bga. Bkwene yaag bmaaduk."

Their staffs descended simultaneously and struck the ground three times, with such force that it cracked the dense gray rock they stood upon.

Everything went quiet.

And then they felt it.

The wind changed direction. It picked up and started to scream. On the water, a wave, like a great hand emerging from the beach, began to roll across the water; the water began to grow into violent swells. Soon the little aluminum boat struggled against crashing white waves.

CHAPTER 21

When Clouds Descend

I must go in, the fog is rising.
Emily Dickinson, poet, d. 1886

"Faster, McBride, give it everything she's got," ordered Norbert.

"It is all she's got!" shouted McBride, over the roar of the motor, the screaming wind, and the chaotic waves.

"It's not enough; they're gaining on us." Norbert's attention was on nine powerful speedboats, hotly pursuing them in a triangular formation.

"We've got to do something," yelled McBride, glancing Nora's way.

Norbert loaded his weapon and looked penetratingly at Nora.

Though no words were exchanged, Nora nodded at Norbert and calmly dropped to her knees, bowing her head as if in prayer.

"Keep her straight, McBride," commanded Norbert as he raised his rifle, waiting for his target to come into range.

With one hand, Khia held on tightly, with the other she cradled her brother closely. The water crashed, the wind swirled, and the boat reeled.

Highly sensitive and attuned to the chaos around her, Nora slowly stood up from her kneeling position and looked like a figurehead frozen in time on a 17th century wooden ship crossing the Atlantic.

"Goa giizaad. Bkwene yaag," Nora chanted.

The wind, driving against them seemed to pause as if to listen.

"Goa giizaad. Bkwene yaag."

In response—the wind stopped. The waves around them calmed and all was perfectly still. The effect couldn't have been more dramatic.

Although Khia had been told to stay under the tarpaulin with Devon, she had to see what was happening.

The sight that greeted her amazed her. No longer bouncing painfully on the crest of every wave, they were gliding on water as smooth and clear as glass. Khia stared wide-eyed as a silvery protective ring encircled them, rippling outwards like skipping flat stones on water.

What kind of powerful Indian magic has Nora invoked? thought Khia.

"Shkang waannishkwaad."

Drawn into the Indian woman's brown eyes, Khia saw that they were turning into the reflection of the glassy water—icy blue. Then Khia watched as a curtain of white began to cloud Nora's eyes, like thick cataracts blocking all sight. Khia turned. On the water, about a thousand feet ahead of them, a sheet of fog rose up.

"Khia, get down. I don't want to have to tell you again," shouted Norbert, as a bullet dinged their boat and he retaliated tenfold.

The furious water had slowed their pursuers as well, but now that the lake was calm, the speedboats rapidly closed in on them.

Just a little farther, thought Khia. *Just a little farther and we can hide in the fog.*

Taking evasive action, McBride threw them hard to the right, a little to the left, and then hard again to the right. The little boat tipped sideways in the water and Norbert reached out to steady Nora. Bullets, coming from their enclosing pursuers, narrowly missed their thin aluminum craft, spraying the water on their port and starboard sides. An array of bombs, shells, and other missiles, painfully close, hit the lake, causing mini water craters to explode into great geysers beside them.

And then McBride took them into the eerie cool world of white fog.

"Bring her to an idle, McBride," ordered Norbert.

Hiding in the protective blanket of mist, they waited.

The fog muffled the sounds. Boat motors and barely audible voices broke through the silence, but they were unable to tell where the sounds were coming from. Fleeting images of boats appeared and disappeared into the fog as if they were apparitions.

Then, as if out of nowhere, two boats from opposite directions headed right towards them. McBride throttled the engine and sped out of the way.

An awful crunch of fiberglass was heard a few feet behind them. A boom and a fireball flashed in the fog. Cries from injured men were heard, as they were flung through the air into the frigid water.

Khia thought she heard other voices in the fog, ancient voices rising up. Khia looked at Nora.

But Nora wobbled. Her outstretched arms trembled from the strain; her eyes fluttered and started to clear. Before Nora collapsed, Norbert sprang to her aid, catching her and gently laying her down.

The fog thinned.

Khia crawled to Nora and placed a blanket over her shivering body.

Placing an ice cold hand on Khia's arm, "They come," she said weakly. "You shall be one." Nora closed her eyes.

As if things couldn't get any worse, Khia heard the sounds of rotor blades before she saw the two helicopters come into view.

Nora lay slumped at the bottom of the boat; Devon remained hidden under the tarpaulin, stealing a peak every chance he could. McBride maneuvered their small boat in a desperate attempt to avoid danger, and Norbert picked up his rifle, raising it towards the heavens and aiming at one of the two Black Hawk helicopters, its rotors moving so fast that they barely seemed to move. The powerful speedboats were circling closer, like sharks coming in for a feeding frenzy.

She had to do something ... but Khia didn't know what to do. The urge to fight rose up within her.

And then time slowed.

Two men appeared in the fog, walking on water. Surrounded in a surreal bluish light, they held out their hands to Nora, but Nora couldn't respond.

Khia rose to her feet.

"K h i a   g e t   D O W N ! !"

She heard Norbert yelling, but his voice sounded far away.

McBride, steering the boat with one hand and holding his Uzi with the other, was also firing. His arm recoiled as its muzzle, in slow-moving frames, belched fire and ejected its silver and gold bullets.

Khia held out her hands, and the two Indian men smiled at her, and took her hands in theirs.

Instantly, Khia entered a different place, somewhat like the dark world Nora had shown her. She could sense their thoughts, and they hers. She was part of a triad—with Rainbow Walker and Grey Horse.

Now she understood. It was Rainbow Walker, Nora's father, who had revealed himself to her in the nursing home. In body they were old and frail, but in spirit they were very powerful shamans.

The ethereal Rainbow Walker winked at her.

In her mind, she could hear and understand, with depth of meaning, the ethereal Grey Horse's words spoken in Ojibwa, "Nkooshmaad nsig zhgong." *The three shall become one.*

And then it became clear what Nora had been trying to teach her.

By their chanting, the fog once again thickened. Before her eyes, fantastic and horrifying images filled the white watery world: ancient legions of warriors, shamans, and totem animals rose up from the fog to do battle.

Khia looked to the bow of the approaching lead boat and saw two Indian shamans. She knew without being told that they were part of the Red Bear Cult. Accelerating towards them, one Indian was covered in red tattoos; the other had his staff raised in the air. Glaring fiercely, the shamans chanted powerful spells and counter incantations. She could hear and understand their words clearly; she could feel their power, their anger, and their hatred.

Hearing the sounds of rotor blades, Khia looked up.

The mechanical beast hovered above the fog. Through the mist, Khia could see the sniper's weapon … its barrel coming down, the sniper's hand squeezing the lethal weapon, taking an unerring aim, with the cross-hairs centered on McBride's head.

Rainbow Walker's voice penetrated Khia thoughts, calming her mind, and centering her.

"Nora has prepared you well. Come, there is a time for everything and now it is time for us to go into battle."

Before the sniper could pull the trigger and release its deadly burst, a great column of fog and vapor rose above the helicopter. Shape-shifting, the column of fog turned into a large, raging, white bear. Rearing up, it struck the helicopter a great blow with its massive paw.

The white bear was instantaneously cut up and shredded by the whirring blades.

The aircraft lurched.

The sniper's shot went wide and she tumbled from the craft.

Dangling from the thin safety tether, she lost her grip and her weapon fell through the air, turning slowly as it fell into the cold watery abyss below.

The pilot heard an unusual thumping sound coming from the engine. Gages flashed and warning horns blared. Black smoke churned out of the exhaust. He called out a distress signal. Followed by the second helicopter, the two aircrafts turned and fled.

But the danger was far from over. Khia watched as the sky turned a boiling red. The two Red Bear shamans would not give up so easily; they had come to fight—to settle old scores that should have been decided eons ago.

The Great White Bear rematerialized along with a Grey Horse.

"Get on my back, Khia," she heard Grey Horse's thoughts. *"We ride ... we will ride into battle."*

Khia leapt onto the horse's back, and euphoria swept over her as she settled into place. A brilliant turquoise fog swirled and rose up around them. Khia instantly recognized Timothea, a great staff in her hands, her eyes aflame with bright energy. From her shadow emerged her black bird, whose wingspan grew and blackened the sky, its wingtips creating swirling vortices. It led the charge, closely followed by its companion, a great shining silver wolf.

As one with the Great White Bear and the Grey Horse, Khia, and Timothea and her totem animals rushed forward ... and with them ancient warriors of the past. Like a great white mass with swirls of turquoise, they assailed themselves against an opposing red tide. The ferocious strength of the Great White Bear crushed and flung aside red warriors and angry beasts as if they were nothing but chafe. Timothea, with her staff, twirled and struck down those who opposed them. The black bird fell upon its prey ripping at them, the Silver Wolf snapping, biting, tearing, and tossing, while ethereal red creatures were kicked and trampled under the hoofs of the Grey Horse.

Before her, Khia saw Norbert's sword materialize in thin air. The sword hung there, an arm's distance away, waiting for her. It had come to her, just as Norbert had said it would, when she needed it most. With a smooth sweep, she took the sword. Listening to its words, she swung it against those who rose up and challenged her.

Hails of red and white arrows soared through the air. Boulders and trees uprooted, flung by ferocious, long-dead shamans. Screaming warriors rushed forward, wild angry nightmarish creatures fought—white and turquoise against red. The water and the sky filled in battle. While on the water, boats crashed and exploded, throwing men around, and casting some into the lake.

Like cornered beasts, the Red Bear shamans fought viciously. Khia felt the hatred of the Red Bear shamans, but she could also clearly see the growing strain on their faces, the sweat beading on their bodies, the fear and doubt … the realization growing in their dark, opaque eyes that they might not be powerful enough.

With deadly effect, they had penetrated the red defenses. Two triads, led by Rainbow Walker and Timothea, were too strong.

Timothea focused her attention on one of the Red Bear shamans. With swift sure strokes and slashes, she struck him … and he fell unconscious onto the deck of the boat.

Above them, the final battle raged between two great bears; a Great White Bear against a Red. The beasts exchanged massive blows, but it was a battle that was both brief and decisive, when the White Bear's jaw closed on the Red Bear's throat. And the second shaman collapsed on the deck of the boat.

They had won; Khia was elated. They gathered, for just a moment, and then the bond was broken. Rainbow Walker and Grey Horse vanished and the turquoise tinge in the fog faded to white.

†

Elation was short lived. "Ohhh," Khia cried out. Everything hurt. She felt achy and sore all over and knew that this was one of the costs for having been within another realm.

Khia looked around at the surreal water-scape. She heard the last of the echoed shots, saw a hundred or so silver and gold bullet casings littering the boat's floor, her brother's pale face peeking out from under the tarpaulin, Nora lying on the bottom of the boat with her eyes starting to flutter open, and the serious faces of McBride kneeling at the stern and Norbert standing at the bow. And then Khia looked beyond and saw the destruction through the wispy curtains of lifting fog. Boats smashed, fires burning, and real men moaning and crying out for help.

"Let's go," said Norbert.

Without comment, McBride started the engine and they weaved through the carnage. None of them spoke. The only act was Norbert's, who threw a red and white life-vest to the outstretched arms of a struggling man as they passed.

CHAPTER 22

The Westmoreland Bridge

Everything passes and vanishes
Everything leaves its trace
And often you see in a footstep
What you could not see in a face.
—William Allingham 1824-1889

Like spawning salmon swimming against the current, they fought their way upstream. About a quarter of the way home, they stopped for fuel cached at an isolated cabin, but there was no time to even stretch their legs before they were on their way again.

Khia remained on the bow of the boat, pensively watching the white world disappear. As the boat passed under a large bridge, she was lulled into a trance. Images haunted her thoughts. She recalled another time, another place.

Khia tensed, and her heart blipped.

Squinting, she turned away from the brilliant sun and looked over at her baby brother, securely fastened in his car seat. They were in the back of a small silver two-door hatchback, which was traveling on a lonely stretch of road that snaked precariously along a mountainous ridge.

Khia's father was driving; beside him (talking amicably) was Khia's beautiful mother, Valerie. Khia's mother glanced back for a moment and smiled at her two children … and Khia saw love and gentleness in her mother's eyes.

They reached the crest of the road; the view was incredible. Before them lay a misted valley, spanned by the Westmoreland Suspension Bridge, and cushioned in soft fog that rolled in from the sea. Farther along, the tops of the bridge towers were visible, giving an illusion that they were moving towards large towering parapets of a hidden castle suspended in the air.

She heard the bump of tires as the car rolled over the bridge plate.

Older Khia tensed. She knew what was coming.

A blur in the car's rear-view mirror caught Khia's attention—a speeding car, only half materialized in the world, as if it were some malignant ghost car stuck between here and somewhere else. Khia watched unblinkingly as it weaved in and out of the unsuspecting traffic and accelerated rapidly towards them.

She knew its malicious intent. Quickly it closed the distance between them. Its tires, on slick wet asphalt, created its own fog, masking its illusionary presence.

The older Khia shouted a warning to her father, but it was futile; he couldn't hear her—couldn't see her. The shadow car struck them; Khia felt it merge with them like a phantom spirit. She gasped and clutched her heart, feeling physical pain as it passed through them and disappeared into the fog.

The steering column twisted out of her father's powerful hands. Khia saw the look of surprise on his face. Desperately, he tried to regain control, but his actions were ineffective. The car wobbled and they skidded sideways, careening to the left. They struck the concrete median hard, and bounced off it, as if they were nothing but a child's spinning toy. In slow painful frames, the car spun and rolled over and over and over. Sparks and glass and steel screamed in protest. The battered car came to a stop. All around, everything seemed possessed of a surreal energetic silence.

The quiet was shattered by the sound of thick heavy rubber being laid down by eighteen pounding wheels—a fully loaded gasoline tanker truck sliding over the slick asphalt and heading straight for their small car, which lay twisted and vulnerable on the bridge.

Through the shattered windscreen, Khia watched in horror as the big rig rose out of the fog like a steel monster. For a split second, as Khia looked through her younger self's eyes, which were locked with the truck driver's, time seemed to stop … with fear reflected, forever frozen, on that truck driver's face.

Reacting, the vehicle jolted and jackknifed. With sickening queasiness, Khia felt and heard the rumblings of the out-of-control tanker as it roared into the concrete median.

The front end struck the barrier with such force that the back end rose high up into the air, swung around, and hit their battered car like a baseball bat hitting a ball.

As though she were in the eye of a hurricane, the older Khia stood quietly in the center of the unfolding chaos. She looked at her younger self, her baby brother, her mother, her father... her family in the crushed car, even as the tanker's first drops of precious liquid escaped, and then started to pour from its badly ruptured tanks—torrents of fuel bursting free like a turbulent river overflowing its banks in the spring. Hundreds of gallons per second, the volatile liquid gushed out, overwhelming the bridge's storm grates, and swirling downwards into the valley below. The silvery-black liquid poured out into the abyss, like from the pitch channels below the buttresses of an impregnable castle.

Another stream of fuel snaked a path around the crushed car, as though it had a mind of its own, enclosing Khia and her family in a silvery-black liquid ring.

The air tasted thick and heavy, a combustible aerosol ... waiting.

The older Khia saw her father imprisoned by crushed steel, plastic, and glass. Blood streaming down his face and in obvious pain, he begged Valerie to save herself and the children.

Calmly, deliberately, Valerie nodded; she unbuckled her seatbelt. She turned and knelt on the front seat, reaching towards her two stunned children in the back. First she removed the restraint from Khia and drew her towards her.

Khia saw her younger self thrust out of the car's busted and bent front window frame.

A moment later, Valerie drew Devon out of his car seat; she kissed him once on the top of his head and placed him in the younger Khia's arms.

Valerie stayed for one last moment with her husband. Smoke was already billowing from the overturned tanker ... Khia watched the last kiss Valerie placed on his lips.

Young Khia stood holding Devon, tears rolling down her face as her father blew her a kiss and mouthed, "I love you. I love you all."

"Go," he gasped, turning to his wife and looking into her eyes, choking back his tears, and his fear for his wife and his children.

"Khia!"

Older Khia snapped her head in the direction where she heard her name called ... but there was no one there!

Scanning the area, her eyes were drawn to a car that was more shadow than real, the car that had struck them on the bridge. The back door opened and a woman stepped out, followed by a young girl who looked to be no more than eight. Older Khia watched silently as the woman placed her hand in a leather satchel and drew something out.

From that distance, older Khia could clearly see the cruel smile etched on her face as she opened her hand and blew a multi-colored, dust-like substance from her palm.

It floated in the air, some kind of a magic pixie dust, creating playful sparkling circles. But then, as if it was tired of its play, it transformed into an angry flame and shot downwards into the Valley below, where air and fuel joined in a nightmarish marriage of oxygen and volatile compounds.

The massive explosion pushed the bridge upwards several feet, causing it to cry out; moments later waves rocked the Westmoreland Suspension Bridge from one end of its foundations to the other, bending, buckling, and swaying upwards and downwards, while many of the rivets that had securely held the steel beams broke like gunshots.

As the bridge slowly settled back into a creaking stillness, Valerie and Khia (still clutching her little brother to her chest) climbed unsteadily to their feet, too numb to feel the various damages done to them by the accident and the bridge's convulsions.

Older Khia watched as her mother took Devon from her younger self, and glanced around, seeming disoriented. She watched as silvery-black fuel splashed over her mother's bare feet, leaving dark footprints behind her as they started walking to safety. Older Khia watched as her mother's elegant footprints slowly lost their shape like footprints in the sand.

Their staggering retreat seemed surreal and endless, but eventually they slowed to a stop, and looked back from a safe distance. They watched, as a thin line of fire emerged on the bridge. Like a snake, it coiled around the truck and grew into a ravenous curtain of flames.

Upright and proud, Valerie watched as the ring of liquid closed in. Trembling, the younger Khia closed her eyes tightly; she did not want to see and only opened her eyes when she felt hot ash and cinders falling like manna from heaven.

Absentmindedly, Valerie placed Devon on the asphalt and walked to the side of the bridge. All about them sections of road and bridge were burning. With glazed eyes, she looked down into the valley. Lost.

Older Khia watched as her younger self silently went over and picked up Devon, cradled the crying child, and rocked him slowly back and forth.

"Come Khia," the woman who had held the pixie dust called out, hypnotically. "Come with me." She held out her hand.

Khia stood immobile … feeling a cold touch on her shoulder, she screamed, "No. NO!"

"Khia!" Another voice penetrated her mind, "It's Nora. Come back."

The images faded and Khia found herself once again on the bow of a small and battered aluminum boat.

Khia gave a sharp involuntary breath. They had just passed underneath the bridge.

"You're safe now," whispered Nora. "You're safe."

"She killed my father," said Khia, with such pain in her voice.

"I know," Nora held Khia tightly in her arms, rocking her gently back and forth. "I know."

CHAPTER 23

The Familiar

One crow sorrow
Two crows joy
Three crows letter
Four crows boy
Five crows silver
Six crows gold
Seven crows for a secret never to be told.

Far far away, in Lady Tiamore's Waterfall Kingdom, a curious creature appeared. At first glance, the creature looked like a small gray cat preening herself under the stone gateway, but if one knew what to look for, and if one knew that sometimes things are not as they appear, one would know that it was not a cat at all, but a Familiar.

This peculiar little gray ball of fur had something astonishingly important to tell, something only known by two others, and of those two, one had never been seen again, and the other had been driven utterly mad, with only faint fragments of recollected memories reverberating hollowly in her damaged mind.

Such a magical creature normally would never have been permitted an audience with the Lady of the Kingdom.

Wary of her claim, the Knight refused her entrance. You see, there had been countless others who had made similar claims, all false, all seeking unwarranted fortune and reward. However, unlike countless others, this curious gray creature was different. It genuinely wanted to tell the Lady its account and leave, while the Knight's intent was only to protect and shelter his Lady from further anguish and pain.

It therefore caught the Knight unaware when he heard soft footsteps behind him. He turned to see his Lady standing at the doorway, holding the Key she always wore on a gold and silver woven chain around her neck. The Key glimmered in the moonlight, reflecting the thousands of waterfalls that marked her kingdom.

Lady Tiamore stood perfectly still. She appeared relaxed and patient, but the Knight, who knew her too well, knew she was uneasy and bracing herself for the inevitable. No doubt, this story too would be false and she would have to face the disappointment and heartache that would surely follow.

With a motion of her hand, she invited the curious creature into her sitting room.

The pseudo cat passed over Lady Tiamore's threshold and instantly transformed into her true form—the form she had been born with: a dark-silver lithe, appearing and disappearing between dimensions, wafting in and out of existence, like whirring, swirling smoke that comes just after a candle has been extinguished.

With no words having yet been exchanged, the Lady knew in her heart—the moment the Familiar stepped over her threshold—that this time she would find the answers she sought, answers she had waited for, for such a long long time.

"Please, make yourself comfortable," spoke Lady Tiamore.

Although anxious to learn the truth, the Knight knew she would not dismiss protocol. Even under the most difficult of circumstances, she was gracious and polite, which she had crafted and perfected over her long lifetime.

"Can I offer you anything? Food or drink?" asked the Lady politely.

"No. Nothing," answered the shimmering creature.

"Tell us then," urged Lady Tiamore.

"My Lady," almost purring, the Familiar began to speak.

†

"Thirty-three earth years ago is when my story starts. It was late and we should have been asleep, but that night my mistress was haunted, awakened by her dreams. Restless, she knew something neared. She sensed it the moment it arrived at our gate. Whatever it was, it was something powerful, and something too awful to name."

The creature looked at Lady Tiamore as if asking for forgiveness. "My mistress was a good woman, perhaps too sensitive, too kind. Willingly, I served her and have a great affection for her even now, after so much has happened and so much time has passed. I have served others less intelligent, less sparing, and less caring." For a moment, the Familiar seemed lost in thought, its edges diffusing.

The creature came back into sharper focus, its colors changing to forest greens with wisps of red. "My mistress knew better than to venture out, and yet she could not resist the sound that called to her. Such was the soft cry, the temptation so great, that it overrode her fear.

"She opened her front door and stepped forth, out into the open air and into the cold mist. Barefoot, she stepped onto the dew-covered stone of the walkway. I followed in her footsteps, wrapping myself around her legs, not wanting her to go.

"But my mistress was not so easily dissuaded; she sought the treasure that lay beyond the gate. As she opened the gate, she stared into the face of a creature that was beyond description—a creature cold, black, and fearful ... a creature that brought death, that brought forth the cold fog that concealed us. In its cloaked arms, it carried a beautiful child with blond hair and big hazel eyes, awake and hungry. It was the sound of the child that had compelled my mistress ... she had such a gentle heart.

"Tenderly, my mistress reached for the child, but the dark creature clasped my mistress' arm in a grip so cold it burned. Being bonded to my mistress, I felt everything: her fear, her pain, her confusion. I felt the shivers sprint up and down her spine, and the cold that penetrated her body to its core. And I felt the desolation and desperation of the creature's voice, which invaded her mind. My mistress gazed into the black void of the Creature's eyes, into its ancient dark soul, had a glimpse of her future, and knew that there were worse things than death.

"'*Woman*,' it rasped, the water vapor from its breath crystallized and broke at their feet like fine glass, '*I know your dreams.*'

"In that moment, my mistress would have turned and run if it was not for the child.

"'*Will you do me a service, woman?*' asked the dark creature. '*Care for this child as your own until I return.*'

"My mistress stared into the child's eyes, and with numb fingers, she accepted the babe and held her protectively to her heart. Deathly afraid to look any longer into the creature's face, my mistress was lost ... for she saw wonders in the child's eyes. She loved this child; she would have given her life for this child ... as would have I.'

"As the creature left us, we heard its warning.

"'*Tell no one,*' it said. Its raspy voice lingered like a malignant potent shadow. '*The life of the child, and yours, depends on it.*'"

"The dark creature never returned," said Lady Tiamore knowingly.

The Familiar nodded. "The secret was kept. But secrets that are never to be told are hard to hold." Although the curious creature could not cry, it showed its strong emotions by shimmering from gold and silver to a charcoal gray. "My Lady, you would have been so proud of her. She was a precious gift. She brought meaning and joy to my mistress. She was wise beyond her years. My mistress taught her all that she knew: knowledge and magic that had been lost to most, remembered by so few.

"Yet dark days will visit us regardless of how we would wish them away. And, the dark day did arrive.

"A stranger visited. My mistress, as was her want, invited her in. You see, my mistress often invited the destitute into her home. For a meal, a wash, a warm bed for the night ... It was her custom, an act of penance. She turned very few away.

"I did not like this woman and hid from her, so she never learned of my existence. But even though my mistress was getting forgetful and care-less as she grew older, she would never have said anything about Valerie had the woman not cast her spell of words. The woman feigned interest and praised my mistress. She said that Valerie, our young lady who had just turned seventeen, was beautiful and certainly a gift from the heavens.

"My mistress admitted that the girl was not her granddaughter and told her she *had* been a gift, not from heaven, but from a creature from a dark world. The moment the secret was released, the spell broke and it was like a foul stain had moved about the room. The mood changed; it was impossible to conceal. My mistress tried to cover the truth of her words, but the damage had been done. The woman, her task accomplished, left ... having never finishing her tea.

"A dark cloud hovered over the house. We chose to tell Valerie as little as possible ... but she knew. Without being told, she knew.

"We prepared for what we knew was rising ominously on the horizon; like a plague, we felt it drawing near. We knew not when or how, but we knew it would arrive.

"A few quiet months passed and my mistress began to dismiss it as imaginings. A mistake, perhaps, but it was easier for her to pretend the woman's visit had never happened, and that there was no danger pending.

"But what is done cannot be undone. The storm struck in the pre-dawn hours. It announced itself with a soft knock at the door. Three times we heard the knock, each one louder than the last. My mistress did not open her door.

"It began with red fireballs flying monstrously through the air; vividly, I remember the dark black trails they left behind. Our windows shattered, our roof began to burn, and poisonous fumes seeped under our landing.

"My mistress tried her best to fight back, but even in her prime, she could never have held them back. They held such power. Trapped in the inferno, Valerie and I went deep underground. My mistress had foreseen such an attack and had prepared an enclosure under the basement floor.

"It was a place where we hoped we could be safe. Valerie and I pleaded with our mistress to come, but so intent was she on protecting Valerie that she did not heed our call. She sacrificed herself for Valerie and the bond with my mistress dissolved.

"It was not long before the sound of the fighting ceased.

"We prayed that they would not find us, but Valerie and I ... we both knew that if they had the skills to so quickly defeat my mistress, it wouldn't be long before they broke the seal of our enclosure.

"Above, we heard the sound of heavy footsteps.

"Valerie ordered me to leave. I begged her to bond with me—familiars are not meant to be alone. She refused. She wanted at least one of us to escape and she knew they wanted her. When the door above us opened, and light flooded into our hiding place, Valerie began her fight. She was strong and fought well. But there were too many.

"As she fell ... I am so sorry, my Lady," the Familiar pleaded, "but I did what no Familiar is allowed; it is forbidden. I forced a bond. I bonded with her without her permission. I was so afraid."

The knight's face was grim.

"For months, I was unable to sense my new mistress, Valerie. When I was able to once again sense her, I was shocked at what I discovered, what they had been forced to endure. My old mistress, poor old Meg, had become a person I did not recognize. Cruelly they had twisted her spirit, tortured her mind, and inevitably she had broken. Valerie, poor Valerie; she had great inner strength and power, but she had been scarred. Great dark lines marred her beautiful face. My Lady ..." the lithe creature paused, its lines shimmering slowly from angry red to cold ice blue, "Valerie was with child."

After a moment, the creature continued. "Anger built up inside me for what had been so cavalierly done. I lay in wait for the day I could help her escape. When she was thick with child, they had grown careless and underestimated her determination. When the moment arrived—when they unlocked her door—we were ready. Valerie wielded such power. The child growing within her made her stronger. They fell before us. Any that hindered us, she slew, and the rest fled. Valerie and I made it through a Portal and back into our mistress' world."

"Throughout the last month of her pregnancy, worry marred Valerie's beautiful face. Terror consumed her about the child she carried. It was then that I detected that she may never fully be healed; her scars were too deep.

"But then Khia was born—three weeks premature—after a very difficult birth. From the moment that Khia was born, Valerie loved her.

"Weakened by the birth, it took many months for Valerie to regain her strength. Valerie, my mistress, took long walks on the beach, carrying her child in her arms. Invisible, I would follow in her footsteps. That's where she met him.

"Immediately, he fell in love with her. For Valerie, it would take much longer. Years. It was he who brought her back from the darkness—the darkness that always threatened to engulf her.

"My dear mistress, Valerie, remained cautious, but there was no need, for he cared for Khia and loved her as his own. When Khia turned six,

Valerie married John Ashworth. She was so happy ... but it was a dark day for me. Valerie said that I had served her well, but she wanted to forget her past. She wanted an ordinary normal life, with John, Khia, and the new baby due within a few months. I could not go against her wishes. She set me free."

The Familiar paused, "And that was the last I saw of my dear mistress, Valerie."

No one spoke for a few moments.

"How did you know where to find me?" asked Lady Tiamore.

"It was your Knight's wanderings, my Lady. Like him, I have wandered long and far. It was by accident, perhaps providence, that in the service of my newest master I learned more. Dragons, whatever form they take, hate knights who desire their treasure of gold and precious gems."

The Familiar stared at the Knight with wonder, "But more do they fear warriors who best them and leave them with unsolved riddles to solve ... a riddle of a dark creature hiding a baby girl so well that even God in his far away Heaven could not find her."

The Knight smiled for the first time, and said, "Asanti."

"Yes, Asanti. I solved his riddle and he set me free. And now that you have heard my tale, I will go back," the lithe creature shimmered a pleasing silver, "for dragons left alone too long can become very cantankerous beings."

The Familiar stood to leave.

"Goodbye, my friend," spoke Lady Tiamore. "You have served well. May the light of heaven always shine on you."

The Familiar sparkled like a display of fireworks. "Goodbye, good Lady," said the Familiar, turning slowly from red to cold blue, for it sensed that, sadly, it was too late for Valerie ... much too late.

The lithe creature left.

"Call Sagar. I wish to speak with her," spoke Lady Tiamore.

Sir Francis looked at Lady Tiamore, more sadness than shock displayed on his face. "You cannot ask her to do such a thing," he said.

She glared at him with real anger in her eyes, anger he had never seen before. "You overstep your bounds, Francis. It is her choice and her choice alone."

"Yes, my Lady," he said. "but … you're getting him involved too."

"He is already involved," she snapped. "We all are!"

Francis bowed a little too rigidly before her and left the room to fulfill her wishes.

Lady Tiamore walked to her window and out onto the balcony for a breath of fresh air. She saw the little creature as it puffed and sparkled, stepping onto the street below. In its stead, a little gray cat walked once again, before stopping for a moment to preen herself. A few seconds later, she made her way along the cobbled pathway, passed the fountain, and disappeared into the garden beyond.

Before disappearing, the peculiar gray cat turned and looked up at Lady Tiamore. She saw the tears that streamed down her face, and thought with sadness that they were like a reflection of the thousands of waterfalls in her kingdom. So much sadness and pain.

Lady Tiamore heard a sharp knock at the door. She wiped her tears and her face looked calm and serene.

A woman entered the chamber and bowed.

Lady Tiamore nodded.

"You called for me, my Lady."

CHAPTER 24

The Sylph

... the Lord will pass over that door and not let the destroyer
come into your houses to strike you down. Exodus 12:23

Death takes on many forms, and over the years, the nursing home had seen its generous share of death ... but the evil that walked in that night was unparalleled.

A little past three, after the night shift nurses had completed their rounds, something evil entered the locked building.

Having followed an erratic path to fulfill its quest, to find and kill a young boy named Devon, the Sylph had left a trail of destruction; dead and dying things had sustained it on its quest. For weeks at a time, it had lost the scent, but it was tenacious.

In the wilderness, it topped a ridge and saw a small aluminum boat riding high in the water, making its way up river. It sniffed the air and knew it had found what it was looking for.

But suddenly it was distracted, and instead of following the child, it turned and went in the opposite direction.

Taking on the human-like form of a slender pubescent girl with long red and gold hair, the Sylph walked down the darkened corridor of the nursing home, silently passing the nurses' station. The duty nurse did not see or hear anything, but the moment it passed, she felt the cold as if the warmth had been sucked away. Unconsciously, she pulled her white sweater around her more tightly.

The elderly residents, many of them in the throws of dementia, felt its presence; some believed it was only a silly hallucination of their aging minds. A few, however, were not so easily fooled, for they had more reason than most to be acutely aware of death's approach. Turning uneasily in their beds, they prayed fiercely that such a bitter angel would pass them by. But it was not seeking them, not on this night. Sometimes death stalks, sometimes death is called, and sometimes death is challenged.

The Sylph stood before room 616B. It heard the weak heartbeats of the two inside. Slowly, it opened the door and saw the bedridden old men in the darkened room.

"Fools," it rasped.

Then it saw two mature men, surrounded in an ethereal glow: one resting lightly against the window pane, his arms folded across his chest a wide grin on his face; the other stood, one foot on the metal railing of his bed, his hands resting on his knee as he looked upon his earthly remaining self.

The Sylph looked at the two shamans. They were not afraid! It was momentarily taken aback, because every encounter it had had in its short life (except for its birth bond with its mother) had been about fear. It had fed on it ... used it. These men had an inner resolve, a quiet power—nothing it could easily exploit.

The door closed. Breaking the silence in the room, its voice reverberated like the low rumbling sounds of distant thunder, "Wizards, why do you call me away from my task?"

The ethereal Grey Horse spoke. "It is unnatural that you walk this earth."

Taking a step towards the ethereal men, it felt the invisible bonds they had placed around it. "Unbind me. Take your ropes from me," demanded the Sylph angrily. Then it laughed, for it understood that these men were weakening, fading from this world. It wouldn't take long to break them. Viciously, it spat, "Weak and old. Pathetic fools."

The lithe creature turned around with an almost magnificent sweeping gesture, and then with the sudden ferocity of a dragon, it launched itself at them.

But the invisible chains held.

Angered, it spat, "Dead, dead, dead. I want you dead."

"Such a petulant child," the ethereal Rainbow Walker taunted the Sylph.

"So young and inexperienced," agreed Grey Horse.

Incensed, the Sylph growled, redoubling its efforts.

"Ah, is it to be a contest of wills?" laughed the ethereal Grey Horse.

"Who is the stronger?" goaded the ethereal Rainbow Walker.

Raging uncontrollably, the Sylph shape-shifted into its original form— the one it had been born with and grown into—that of a powerful beast with fangs, and muscles alive with youthful vigor.

"Who is the smarter?" asked the ethereal Rainbow Walker.

Acutely aware, the Sylph changed tactics. Containing its anger, it focused its strength on the ethereal ropes that held it … and saw them start to fray.

The ropes snapped and the Sylph burst forward. With a clawed fist, it struck through the ethereal Rainbow Walker with such force that the hospital equipment that had been behind him smashed to the floor. The ethereal men faded and disappeared.

Looking at the two old men in their beds, it couldn't understand what strange magic they had used to summon it. The Sylph bent down. "Old dried meat," it growled like a hungry lioness. Its hot saliva dripped and burned the sheets. "Time to die."

That's when the door to room 616B opened.

Nurse Beverly dropped the contents of her metal tray, and screamed.

Except for the helpless in the adjacent rooms, no one heard, for Nurse Beverly was the only staff member assigned to the 6th floor.

The Sylph growled and barred its teeth.

Nurse Beverly, of Haitian ancestry, had never seen a Sylph before, but she recognized evil when she saw it. But fear alone would not cause her to flee, for Nurse Beverly protected those under her care.

With a loving woman's heart, and loathing in her eyes, she attacked. Using the metal tray as a shield, she faced the creature like a Knight.

With a great cuff, the Sylph backhanded the woman and sent her careening into the corner, the tray clattering to the floor.

Nurse Beverly, not so easily dissuaded, picked up her tray and wavered to her feet. Unsure as to what to do, she reached out desperately for anything. In the darkened room, her hands clasped a water jug and she threw its contents at the creature.

The creature screeched in pain. The water burned its saffron skin.

"Run fast creature of fire, lest you miss what you are searching for," said the ethereal Rainbow Walker, so that only the Sylph could hear.

"Devon," screamed the Sylph in frustration. These weak pathetic old men had veered it away from its quest. It had been tricked, tricked into fighting them, taking it away from its true goal. They had distracted it ... confused it. How?

An invisible force plowed into it and it was pushed across the floor towards the window. As it was pushed through the window, glass shattered into thousands of pieces.

Falling six stories, tumbling through the air, it screamed with poisonous venom, "Devon! Kill Devon!"

Landing on the ground, the Sylph rose uninjured. Sniffing the air, the creature resumed its mission, catching the scent of the child and running towards the lake, faster than the wind.

"Devon!" the Sylph screamed.

Miles away a sleeping boy stirred.

†

Nurse Beverly looked out the broken window, but couldn't see anything; it was too dark. She had no doubt, however, that the creature she had seen would easily survive the fall.

On a piece of glass sticking out of the window pane, she saw a small amount of burning blood. In the next instant it vaporized, as if it had never existed.

Taking a deep breath, she walked tentatively towards her two elderly charges.

Lying in bed, wide awake, Grey Horse smiled, "Nurse Beverly, you are a true warrior."

Nurse Beverly didn't know how to respond and so said nothing. Her feet crunching on broken glass, she slowly approached Rainbow Walker, afraid of what she might find. She covered a gasp with her hands. Tubes had been ripped from him; damaged machinery beeped uselessly.

She touched his carotid artery, to feel for a pulse; it was faint but he was alive.

Carefully replacing his tubes, she looked at him with compassion. *He looks so frail*, she thought. His eyes were closed, but she detected a hint of a smile on his face—the first sign of emotion that she had seen from him in a long long time.

She didn't know how or why, but she knew that the frail and elderly resident of room 616B wasn't ready to die. Not yet. It was like there was something yet for him to do.

CHAPTER 25

The Planes of Abraham

The household was up early. Khia was tired, but she knew the routine and completed her chores without being asked. She made the bed, fed the two dogs, and sat at the breakfast table.

McBride produced a great feast. Their fare included fresh eggs, toast, and bacon, along with pancakes and the sweetest maple syrup Khia and Devon had ever tasted. Sadly, it reminded Khia of their last meal at the Brislings.

When they had finished eating, Khia started to clear up, but Nora stopped her. Leaving the dishes, Nora took her aside so they could talk privately.

"Khia, I will miss you," she began. "I have enjoyed your company, and so have my dogs. Sometimes, I think they know better than I who I can trust." Nora's tone changed and she became much more serious. "It's no longer safe here. You and your brother must leave."

"I know," she replied. Even though she had been expecting it, her breath caught; Khia had gotten attached to Nora and liked this isolated place, deep in the wilderness. They'd been here for weeks, their stay longer than at any of their foster homes, and she had started to believe that this was a place they could stay—a place where they could call home.

"You will be meeting my son soon. He's going to take you a little closer to your grandmother's. Go pack your things," Nora shooed Khia away, so that she wouldn't see her tears.

Feeling sad and lonely, like she'd felt so many times before, Khia gathered her few possessions.

It wasn't long before she found herself sitting in the truck beside her brother, making their way to the river with the two dogs running along excitedly.

As they reached the river's edge, the sun burst over the horizon, just as a high-powered twin-engine float plane appeared over their heads, skimming the trees.

"Have you ever been in an airplane before?" Nora asked.

"Many times," replied McBride.

"Not you," Nora shook her head and laughed.

The float plane landed on the water and taxied into view, and for a moment, it looked as if it were a speed boat on the misty river. A dozen or so feet from them, it slowed and settled more deeply into the water. With a tight turn and a sudden burst of power, it beached itself on the sandy bank. The pilot killed the engine and the propellers came to a chugging stop.

Nora's son exited the plane. He was an attractive man with playful eyes and a big smile. Although younger, Khia thought he looked very much like the ethereal Rainbow Walker.

The young man shouted, "Uncle Norbert. McBride."

The two dogs rushed into the water and swamped him with their affection. Once back on dry land, the dogs shook themselves, and water sprayed everywhere.

Devon laughed cheerily.

The man reached out to Norbert, but instead of taking the handshake he offered, he was taken into the great arms of Uncle Norbert, who lifted him off the ground in greeting; McBride tussled his hair as if he were still a young buck.

"And where's mine," interrupted Nora.

"Hello mother," he said seriously, with a slightly abashed look, avoiding the blast (that he knew through experience) was coming. "I know, I know," he said, before Nora could say anything, "why don't I visit more often and bring the kids."

Frantically searching his vest's many pockets, he continued, "Yeah, but mother—"

"Don't give me any yeah buts," Nora said, her eyes narrowing.

At last he found what he was looking for and drew forth the precious items from deep within hidden places. "I come bearing gifts," he said triumphantly. "I bring photographs and drawings."

He proudly displayed objects made by his two daughters, keenly demonstrating the wisdom of a son who had felt the love, and the furies, of Indian wives, mothers, aunts, and grandmothers.

That was of course all that Nora needed, photos of her granddaughters that showed how much they had grown and drawings that showed that their grandmother was still in their thoughts, as well as in their hearts. Beaming, Nora took these things and was lost to them.

"New recruits?" he looked at Norbert and McBride questioningly.

"Hello," he introduced himself. "The name's Abraham, but most of my friends just call me Abra, as in Abra-ka-da-bra." He shook hands with Khia and Devon, who introduced themselves shyly to the man.

He turned to his mother and said, "You called."

"My mom," Abraham said with pride, looking at Khia and Devon, "has a very unique way of calling me. My mom can't be normal and call me on the phone like other mothers; no she calls me in my thoughts and in my dreams no less … and just to make sure, she invades my Aunt Flora's sleep, who uses more conventional methods and will call me and e-mail and text me a dozen or more times to make sure that I get the message," he laughed.

"I had to rearrange some things but—" suddenly he was distracted by the truck. "Hey, Mom is that your new truck?"

Nora nodded with a twinkle in her eyes. "It is now."

He shook his head, "I don't know how you do it. But then again, Uncle Norbert and McBride ... okay don't tell me." He turned to the two Ashworths and (digressing) said, "You know, my first time, it was Uncle Norbert and McBride who—"

"Place and time, Abra," responded Norbert.

"Okay, okay. What's up? Why the urgency?" He looked around at all the glum faces and then something suddenly clicked in his head. He looked at Khia, then at Devon, and back at Khia more closely. "Oh no!" he said slowly. "Two kids. Oh, no. No!" he said, with even more emphasis. "Two kids, ohhhhhh!" he repeated, as he put the pieces together. "Everyone in the territory is looking for you. You guys are more notorious than Bonnie and Clyde blasting across the country. Carnage at the border, churches burning, clips of you disappearing into the fog with boats and helicopters in hot pursuit … That boat … I thought I recognized that boat. That's MY boat!

"Uncle Norbert, McBride, Mother," he said in a reprimanding voice. "What on earth have you been up to? A little discretion perhaps."

"Not our style," McBride offered weakly with a smile.

"I should have known," said Abraham, "the three amigos reunited once again." He shook his head.

No one said a word.

Then Abraham smiled, "The footage on the news was incredible."

"Would have liked to have seen that. What clip did they use?" asked McBride.

"We don't have time, McBride," Norbert interrupted.

"And now I'm involved," continued Abraham. "The wife is going to kill me when she finds out. Just as well you used a dream to contact me, Mom," he said philosophically.

"We promise we won't tell," retorted McBride, with a playful chuckle.

"What do I have to do?" Abraham asked, not able to hide his eagerness. "I haven't had an adventure like this in a long long time. Well, actually, not since the last time Norbert and McBride paid us a visit. You should really visit more often."

Nora took her son aside.

†

Sounding more like a cowboy than an Indian, Abraham shouted to McBride and Norbert, "Let's load it up!"

"Already done," said Norbert.

"While you were talking to your Mom," said McBride.

Their goods and the assortment of weapons were neatly packed in the small plane.

"Goodbyes are so difficult," said Nora.

Nora hugged Khia close for a few precious seconds. She whispered, "I hope to see you again."

Abraham gave the dogs a rough but playful farewell, and his Mom a parting hug. He gave the plane a mighty push, and it caught the river's slow current and began a slow lazy turn. He jumped onto the pontoon.

"Abraham," shouted Nora, "you deliver them safely, you hear. That's all that matters: those two kids."

Amid furious barking, Abraham climbed into the cockpit.

Putting his seatbelt on and locking the door securely, Abraham checked his gages, and completed his starting procedures.

"Seatbelts on. If you feel sick, we have sick bags," said Abraham.

With a last look and a wave to his mother, Abraham started the engine. In his hands, it came alive and everyone aboard felt that the plane was imbued with an eager anticipatory energy—this was a plane and pilot that loved and wanted to fly.

Abraham gave the plane some throttle and the plane taxied away, leaving Nora, the truck, and the two dogs behind.

"We're off!" shouted Devon gleefully.

The plane accelerated, and like a fast boat, Khia felt it skim across the water. They made their way up river until they came to a long open stretch of water. Abra gave the plane full throttle. Accelerating, the plane banked lightly to one side lifting one pontoon out of the water, banked the other way, and then they were in the air only a few feet above the water.

Devon felt sick the moment the plane lifted off. "I don't feel so good."

Norbert and McBride put it down to airsickness, since the kid had never been in a plane before. McBride opened the vent, which gave him cooler air, and passed him the sick bag.

Khia looked ahead and saw the trees rapidly approaching. Just as she was wondering if the plane would clear the trees, Abraham pulled the plane's steering column hard and they went zooming above them. Efficiently, he accomplished a one hundred and eighty degree turn, aligned them with the river, and they sank back below the tree line heading back over Nora's property.

Expecting to see his mother enthusiastically waving up to them, he was shocked at what he saw.

All around Nora were shattered, burning trees. They were horrified to see that only one of her dogs stood by her side barking and growling furiously, its fangs barred viciously. The other, Zipper, had already been struck down.

Khia pressed her nose flat against the plane's Plexiglas window; she saw the terrible creature Nora faced: an angry animal that cannot be imagined except perhaps in mythical stories of beasts from a hellish world.

Devon felt a sudden searing pain.

Khia's eyes made contact with the beast, distracting it momentarily from Nora. In that brief moment, Khia was aware that this was no dumb beast but an intelligent creature, born to kill. Khia was also able to read the creature's thoughts and emotions. Hatred festered inside the creature and it wanted Devon dead.

It screamed a horrible other-worldly scream that seemed to buffet the plane with its fury. Ripping a branch from a large burning tree, the limb burst into a bright, angry yellow flame. In a mighty swish, it threw the heavy beam as if it were a spear. Abraham threw the craft downwards and almost instantaneously jerked it upwards, evading the lethal missile by inches. The burning shaft passed harmlessly by.

Nora used that critical moment and counterattacked with a berserker's fury.

"We have to help her," screamed Khia.

Norbert, sitting beside Nora's son, placed his powerful hands onto the steering column, steadying the death-grip Abraham had on his aircraft. Abraham, pale with fear for his mother, looked at Norbert and nodded wordlessly, remembering the words that his mother had spoken to him only a few minutes before: '*You deliver them safely, you hear. That's all that matters: those two kids!*'

Abraham banked his plane to take the next contour of the winding river. Khia pressed herself even more tightly against the clear glass, tears of frustration clouding her vision. She watched as the beast attacked and Nora fell. It was the last thing she saw.

Topping a ridge, they saw the intense, towering forest fire. The inferno spread, fed on the drought-ravaged forest. Great plumes of smoke, like volcanic ash, billowed skywards. The horizon was already smothered in smoke and sheets of flame—a fire that even Hell would have been envious of.

Then they saw a flash.

"Over there," pointed McBride.

Miles away to their port side, flying in formation barely above the trees, a phalanx of seven black military helicopters appeared.

Avoiding detection, Abraham flew dangerously low—below the tree line.

"But Nora," Khia cried, pressing her pendant so hard into her palm that her skin turned red and left an imprint of the white bear claw.

CHAPTER 26

Safe Houses

Flying underneath hydro lines and old decrepit bridges, they followed the meandering river. Taking a few detours over ridges and escarpments, they traced other rivers and tributaries, taking the long way and eventually landing on a small lake hundreds of miles away.

Taxied into a protected slip, Abraham turned off the engine.

"How long do we have to wait?" asked McBride.

"Long enough to know that it's safe, and that no one followed us," replied Abraham.

"We taught him well, eh McBride?" Norbert nudged his buddy.

Sometime later, a light that was reflected on the water flashed on and off three times. Abraham responded in a predetermined code.

Moments later, they heard the sound of another float plane. It emerged like a silver ghost gliding on water.

A quick transfer was carried out by McBride. Norbert hung back and spoke to Abraham. "She's a strong woman," said Norbert somberly.

Abraham nodded.

"Go to your wife and children."

"Yeah, but—"

"Then be careful," Norbert interrupted, knowing that Abraham wouldn't be taking his advice, and knowing that, if he had been in his place, he wouldn't have either.

"Norbert, we gotta go," said McBride quietly.

Norbert gave Abraham a quick hug and boarded the plane.

As they flew off, Khia looked out the window and watched Abraham. He stood on the pontoon of his plane, waving at them, alone in the wilderness, with the setting sun behind him looking like a giant ball of fire.

†

In the middle of the night, dim battery-operated lights guided their landing onto a short dirt runway. Once they had landed, the lights were quickly extinguished, leaving them in complete darkness.

They were on the northern edge of an Indian reservation that straddled the Canadian and United States border. Undetected, they slipped across the American border and arrived at a small cabin where an old native woman awaited their arrival.

†

That same night, after the kids were asleep, Norbert and McBride switched on the news. The news reported an unprecedented late-season forest fire that had consumed thousands of hectares of boreal forest. Norbert and McBride looked at the aerial pictures of the raging inferno. Neither said anything, but both were thinking of Nora, and wondering if anyone could have survived such an inferno.

Norbert turned off the television.

McBride broke the dour silence. "We leave first thing in the morning. We have to get the kids through the Portal."

Grimly, Norbert nodded.

†

Overnight, Devon developed a very high fever.

The native woman, using traditional herbal remedies, had difficulty keeping the young boy's fever down. Unaware that Khia was awake and listening, she said solemnly to Norbert and McBride, "This fever is not natural. You can't move him, at least for a few days. He must rest."

Norbert and McBride took a short stroll outside to discuss the situation. After some debate, they decided that they would leave in the morning.

As scheduled, a vehicle arrived to pick them up. An older, somewhat frail, white woman named Emily was at the wheel. She had sad blue eyes and fading blond hair that had started to turn gray.

In the backseat, Devon, wrapped in a blanket, laid his head on Khia's lap. Wordlessly, they left the Indian world behind.

As they drove away, it started to rain. Emily turned on the windshield wipers. For hours, Khia silently stared at the droplets of rain being swept away by the squeak of the wiper blades.

Hours later, they pulled into the driveway of a modest house in a residential area. They pulled into the garage and the door closed behind them.

"One night," said Norbert.

Emily conceded.

But Devon's condition worsened.

For three days and three nights they remained indoors with curtains drawn. Khia felt tense; she could sense the forces set against them closing in. She knew that if they waited too long in any one place bad things would happen.

Bored and restless, Khia pulled out an old photo album from a dust-free shelf. She opened the album and discovered old black and white photographs. One caught her attention: a much younger Emily holding Norbert's hand. "Odd," thought Khia, noting how Norbert hadn't aged a day. The only difference was that he didn't have a scar on his face.

A cough behind Khia interrupted her.

Guiltily, Khia startled.

"Photographs, they can tell us a lot." Emily took the album away from Khia and said, "Come. We're leaving."

†

At four p.m., they backed out of the driveway.

By seven p.m., they could see the lights of New York City on the horizon.

By seven-fifteen p.m., they were trapped.

"Damn," swore Norbert. "It's like they know our every move even before we do."

For the first time ever, Norbert and McBride had been caught unprepared … or perhaps they had known and simply let things unfold as they were meant to unfold.

Trusting Emily, they had missed some obvious clues. Typically, McBride would have driven, but Emily had insisted on driving. She had driven slowly, had checked the rear-view mirror frequently, and then had looked at her watch. Pulling over onto the side of the road, she gave a lame excuse about needing to inspect the engine, claiming it was running hot. She hadn't wanted Norbert or McBride to help, stating they should remain in the car. With the hood up and the keys in her pocket, unmarked cars and Military Special Services surrounded them. With the kids in the back, they had no place to run. Nothing (or so they thought) had been left to chance.

"I'm sorry," Emily whispered to Norbert, tears flowing down her face, "I had no choice."

"We always have choices," said Norbert bitterly.

†

At the scene, a well-intentioned psychiatrist was convinced that the children were suffering from some kind of Stockholm syndrome, where the victims display loyalty to their captors. She tried to calm them. She assured them that they were safe, and that things were going to be all right now that they were away from those two bad men. She led them towards a gray Hummer.

Khia looked back and saw Norbert and McBride handcuffed, and orange hoods thrown over their heads—treated like terrorists. They were roughly thrown into a steel-reinforced van.

Not listening to the psychiatrist, Khia's eyes veered towards a large black limousine that had pulled up. She watched curiously. The back door opened and a very young girl, no more than five, stumbled out.

The little girl looked scared and disoriented. Khia didn't see who was in the car, but saw someone shove the little girl in the right direction. Clinging tightly to a plush toy, she ran to Emily … who knelt down to embrace her, crying openly, because at last, her grandchild was safely in her arms.

†

Colonel Patrick Summer, a veteran of Vietnam, Panama, and the First and Second Gulf Wars, was speaking on a secure line.

"Yes. We have apprehended the two men. They are in custody," Summer replied. "No, they won't be going anywhere."

Khia listened attentively. Although she couldn't hear the speaker on the other end of the line, it wasn't difficult to figure out what and who they were talking about.

Then there was silence. Khia watched as Colonel Summer nodded.

"We followed Mr. Elliot's instructions. They are by my side."

And then Khia faintly heard a single word.

"They."

It came out muffled, but she knew it was the voice of a woman.

A shiver ran up Khia's spine.

"Yes, the girl and her brother," Colonel Summer answered and quickly explained the next stage of their operation. "The convoy is leaving as we speak. At the Long Island Coast Guard Facility, the two prisoners will be transported," he paused aware that Khia was listening, "to a larger and more secure location."

Colonel Summer casually looked out of the Hummer's window. He spotted an animal that he thought was a stray dog.

It was no dog.

Hell had visited Colonel Summer many times in his career. He had seen men die. He had ordered men to their deaths in places euphemistically called theaters. He himself had been an active actor on such stages and had faced impossibly grim situations.

He dropped the phone.

The woman on the other end of the line cursed. But no one heard. The thing that she had been instrumental in resurrecting had interfered at the wrong time in her plans.

The line went dead.

Hell visited Colonel Summer again that day, and showed him what a poor job he had done in this life.

The dog-like creature moved from vehicle to vehicle, haphazardly crushing steel and bullet-proof glass like it was tinfoil and fine crystal. In its anticipatory zeal to find Devon, it destroyed anything and everything in its path, ripping men and vehicles apart like they were stuffed animals and toy cars.

Burning saliva dripped from its mouth, causing the ground to smolder in patches. Unable to contain its excitement, it slashed at the next vehicle, a van, and cleaved it in half.

"Opportunity. It is a mysterious thing," said Norbert, escaping their confinement. Already the hoods were off their heads and the unlocked chains falling at their feet.

"Who would of thunk it? We have that thing to thank," said McBride.

"Get over it, McBride, 'cause it's heading right for Khia and Devon."

The convoy was in chaos—military vehicles crashed, burned and exploded, and blood splattered everywhere. It resembled a war zone.

No one noticed Norbert or McBride.

Tracers and bullets ricocheted off bullet-proof glass and steel-plated Hummers. They had no defenses against this unexpected and unknown onslaught.

The large Hummer carrying Khia and Devon had gone off the road and flipped onto its side. The creature pounced onto the vehicle with a loud thump. There was the sound of several inches of steel and metal being torn asunder.

The Sylph ripped the door of the Hummer from its anchor, and launched it (along with the driver) into the air like a Frisbee.

At point-blank range, Colonel Summer emptied six rounds from his pistol into the creature's face. Bullets were as harmless as throwing confetti into the air.

Then the Sylph retaliated.

Colonel Summers, with his 200-pound frame, was thrown spiraling into the air like a football. His destiny, a quiet grave in Arlington, imminently waited.

"Devon," the Sylph eyed its prize and gave a triumphant scream, breathing in the aroma of the young boy, a scent it had followed across a continent.

Khia didn't know what to do except to shield her brother with her body. Huddling at the farthest part of the overturned Hummer, she knew it wouldn't be long. She wasn't strong enough to attack the Sylph, but it would have to reach in and get her first.

The creature spat, "Devon." It was so close that Khia could feel its hot breath burning her face. "Devon."

She braced herself. There was no escape.

And that's when a missile, fired from a shoulder-mounted rocket and let loose by one of two really pissed-off men, hit the creature and filled it with unbelievable pain. It wouldn't be nearly enough to kill the creature, but it was enough to disable it for a few precious seconds. Tipped with depleted uranium, the missile bit deeply into the creature's flank, and radioactive isotopes coursed through its bloodstream.

The creature landed with a terrific whomp. Its splattered blood created a sheet of fire all around it. Unable to move, it could only watch as Devon and the girl were pulled from the burning vehicle. And it watched as they ran towards another Hummer and sped away.

The Sylph felt the bones within it knitting and mending. It stumbled and screamed in frustration. Serrated shrapnel, embedded deep within it, was expelled. But the creature did not begrudge the pain, for it knew that in only minutes it would be healed. Elated, it smiled, for already bullets were flying towards it, men converging on it ready to do battle. It would have the taste of blood and there would be time ... there would be time for it to pursue its victim. It would never stop.

†

Six time zones away, a soft knock awoke an aging man who had given strict orders for his clergy to inform him immediately of certain developments in the world.

"Padre Eterno. Lo e come abbiamo timore." *It is as we have feared.*

CHAPTER 27

Stalk and Strike

"And what took you so long," reprimanded Khia, sounding all grown up.

"Well, little Miss, we got here as soon as we could," Norbert drawled.

Khia leaned over and gave him a big hug. "I was so scared," she said, sounding like a little girl again.

"Are you blushing?" laughed McBride.

"Concentrate on your driving," glared Norbert.

In their damaged military vehicle, with one door missing and the windscreen shattered like a jigsaw puzzle, the four of them advanced pinball-style to New York City.

When they reached the city, McBride pointed to a sobering development. The heavy traffic was slowing them down.

"I think we might have to try that tube thing Norbert," suggested McBride.

"McBride, you know I hate confined underground spaces," scowled Norbert.

"Ah, they're not so bad," answered McBride.

"After the kind of mess you got us into last time?" exclaimed Norbert. "Remember it was me who dragged your sorry ass out."

"Now, now Norbert, why don't you admit it; you're afraid of the dark."

"I am not afraid of the dark."

"You are."

"Am not. It's just that something bad always happens in underground places. Why? Can you answer that for me?" asked Norbert.

"Unfortunate coincidences. Not likely to happen again," dismissed McBride.

"You're not helping," the large man retorted, his voice tensing noticeably.

Their vehicle came to a lurching stop.

Gridlock.

"Damn," swore McBride, striking the steering wheel in frustration and bending it noticeably.

"How close are we to the Por ... meeting place?" asked Norbert, desperately trying to come up with an alternate plan—anything to avoid the bowels of New York.

"Not far," answered McBride.

A knock on the window caused Khia to turn ... and see the last people in the world she expected to see.

"Norbert, McBride ... are you just going to wait there with your mouths open, or are going to let us in?" asked Goula, smiling. Beside her stood her Irish partner, Dodger, who winked at Devon and Khia.

"Good to see you again Khia and Devon," he called out to them. "Like I always say ... friends are always destined to meet again."

"How'd you find us?" asked Norbert.

"It wasn't difficult," laughed Dodger. "You've been a little conspicuous, I'd say."

The light turned green and Goula and Dodger jumped into the vehicle. In a flash, McBride (taking little notice of other vehicles on the busy street) put his foot on the accelerator and made a U-turn. Following Dodger's directions, he went east two hundred yards and then parked the beat-up military vehicle half on and half off the curb.

"They're close. Very close," Goula told them as she took clothing out of a big bag. "Khia, Devon, I need you to take your clothes off and put these on. The Kevlar vest goes under your jacket."

A bullet proof vest! How much more danger are we in? thought Khia.

"Dodger thinks that the thing that is following you is attracted to your scent. We'll take your old clothes to try and draw the beast away," informed Goula.

Dodger updated Norbert and McBride as to how events were unfolding, while he handed them weapons—guns and knives—that they tucked away in all kinds of interesting places.

"And you'll be taking these," said Dodger, in his Irish brogue. At their feet were two large duffel bags filled with an arsenal of weapons.

"It's not safe, but you already know that. Everyone and their aunt and bloody dog are looking for you." Dodger paused, "And in case you didn't know, we have confirmation that Blackwood is involved."

"That's bad ... real bad," said McBride.

"Expect Blackwood mercenaries to be waiting for you."

"On the bright side, Goula and I have been busy. We've set up a few little surprises for them along the way. It will add to the confusion and give you a little time. Did you like the pandemonium we caused at the border? We crashed the computers on 'em; it was Goula's idea. Beautiful and brilliant," he smiled.

"So it was you," commented McBride. "Nice work. Very nice work."

"You'll have to take the underground." Dodger looked directly at Norbert. "Goula will work her magic and get you through the metal detectors."

Norbert remained silent.

"No more time, Dodger. They have to go," Goula smiled encouragingly at them and gave the two kids, now dressed in dark blue and green hoodies, a quick hug. "Be brave. You're almost at your grandmother's door."

Ten seconds later, Goula and Dodger squealed off in the damaged Hummer, leaving them alone on the streets of New York.

"Let's hope this plan works," commented Dodger, throwing an article of Khia's and Devon's into a garbage truck going in the opposite direction. He squeezed his wife's arm, but already her fingers were busily typing on the laptop computer; she didn't see but sensed the worried look that was on his face.

†

Briskly, they walked towards the subway. Norbert stopped dead at the top of the stairs, paralyzed with fear.

Khia, already halfway down, stopped and stared up at him in disbelief. "What's the matter Norbert?" Khia didn't think that Norbert could be afraid of anything.

"I really hate dark underground places," he answered truthfully.

"Do you want to hold my hand?" asked Devon, holding up his hand.

Norbert smiled, took Devon's hand, and they walked down the stairs together.

Reaching the bottom step, Norbert whined, "McBride, this is not a good idea. I've got a bad feeling about this."

"Oh for God's sake, Norbert, come on. Don't be a baby," McBride said, reprimanding him. "What could possibly happen?"

"Damn, I hate you, McBride," swore Norbert under his breath, but he followed.

It could have been Norbert's awkwardness, the bulges that concealed their weapons, the heavy duffel bags they carried, or the fact that they were two men with two kids. It is a truism that sometimes fate works for you and sometimes against. Regardless, as the four of them walked through the turnstiles, one of the toll attendants, Jimmy M (who had been born in Hong Kong and immigrated to New York City decades ago), noticed. Something struck him as odd. He motioned to his coworker.

As they disappeared onto the platform, Jimmy sifted through his old newspapers. Near the bottom of the pile he found what he was looking for: a picture. It was faded and there was a stained coffee cup ring on it, but you could clearly see the picture of the boy and the girl who had been abducted. The image sent shivers deep into his marrow. He picked up the phone, his fingers shaking, and called Transit Security; he was put on hold.

Seven minutes passed before the train arrived. On the platform, Norbert and McBride avoided the cameras. It was an excruciating wait.

Norbert felt another ring closing in around them.

†

To Khia, the sounds of the steel wheels on the tracks sounded like an inhuman scream of a creature from another world.

On the train, Khia watched silently as a woman and her young daughter sat opposite them. The young girl, perhaps five, smiled shyly at Khia and then turned quickly towards her mother. The little girl chatted lively to her mother and Khia saw the love in the woman's eyes. It reminded Khia of when she was little. She missed her mom.

Unknowingly, this mother and child, and everyone else on the train, were in imminent danger ... because of them. A cold realization reverberated through her. Danger.

"Norbert," Khia whispered anxiously.

Her guardian looked at her.

"It's not safe. I can feel it."

Norbert nodded. "I feel it too."

Arriving at the next station, the train slowed. Norbert looked at the swirl of faces through the glass and recognized a face in the crowd.

"McBride, an old acquaintance of ours has made an appearance."

McBride wasn't surprised.

The whistle blew. The doors closed.

McBride watched.

On the platform, Burdock ran towards the train, but the doors closed before he could get on. Burdock, in anger, banged his fist against the fleeing train.

In the tunnel, between stations, the lights went out and the train came to a screeching stop.

By this time, Jimmy M was back on hold at Transit Security.

"We've got to get out of here now," demanded Norbert.

McBride agreed.

Norbert savagely pried the doors open; they jumped onto the tracks and into the windy black tunnel.

Making their way along the main tunnel, they turned left and entered the maze. Underground tunnels and tributaries led them deeper into older sections and into the bottom of the heart of Manhattan.

Norbert stopped. A bricked-up space with rusted iron bars lay a few feet above their heads. The large man ripped the bars from their rusted mooring. Without consultation, he picked up Khia and Devon and almost threw them through the small opening. As McBride prepared to follow, a voice he knew only too well shouted out to them in the darkness.

"The last time we met, I left you for dead."

"Told you so, McBride," said Norbert. "Hello Burdock," growled Norbert. He planted his feet firmly on the ground, clenched his fists, and faced his arch-nemesis.

CHAPTER 28

Between Heaven
and Hell

"Nice scar, Norbert," mocked Burdock.

"Gives me character," said Norbert, as he grabbed McBride's shirt, holding him back.

But like a Jack Russell terrier, yapping, McBride interjected, "You're scum. You should have died a long time ago. It would be my pleasure to make sure it happens this time."

"Ah McBride," Burdock spoke condescendingly, "you should remember your place. You remember that special place that's reserved just for you in Hell. It will be my pleasure to escort you back to where you belong ... more or less in one piece."

"McBride, go," said Norbert sharply to his friend, knowing he was no match for the one they faced.

"You should be more careful with the company you keep, Norbert," laughed Burdock.

"And you," countered Norbert.

Burdock snarled and stepped from the shadows. His sword glinted darkly.

Khia, hiding in the passage above, heard its call. It was, she realized, a sword like Norbert's, only blacker, darker. Instead of welcoming her, like

Norbert's sword had done, it wanted to harm her, taste her blood, and slowly drain her of life. Khia held onto her brother's hand a little tighter.

"It calls for you, Khia. Can you hear it?" Burdock sneered. "Can you hear it?"

Khia couldn't see his face, but his voice chilled her.

"I'll meet you up above," said McBride to Norbert.

Once McBride had climbed through the hole, he grabbed hold of Khia and Devon and led them along the dark passages. "No dithering," he said to them.

"What does dithering mean?" asked Devon.

"No shilly-shallying."

"Shi—"

"No time to explain. Move!" he said, much more roughly than he wanted to.

†

"It's been a long long time since my steel has tasted untainted blood," derided Burdock.

"And it'll be a longer time still," replied Norbert.

"Tell me brother," said Burdock, as he and Norbert circled each other in the enclosed space, "do you even know who it is you protect? Do you know what the girl can do for us?"

Norbert drew out his sword.

Burdock chuckled, "You don't know!"

The echoing sound of Burdock's laughter turned into the sound of ringing steel as the two of them savagely threw themselves at each other.

A terrific volley of thrusts, parries, and spars marked their meeting. Equally matched in skills honed through the centuries, each shared an eternal hatred for the other. Their blades locked, sharing their masters' living wraths.

Stalemate.

"You do not speak," Burdock grunted in a patronizing voice, as if talking to a disobedient child. "You are so easy to deceive; you always took things at face value—one of your many failings. Your scrumptious little morsel, Ms Percival, failed to mention the importance of the children you protect?"

At the sound of Ms Percival's name, Norbert threw himself with renewed vigor at his antagonist, but Burdock threw him off.

"Such misguided devotion," spoke Burdock, sounding as if he were enjoying himself. "Intcresting how I was always able to read you. You've lost. The Three Kingdoms are no more. Ezrulie ... well you know that Ezrulie turned sides, and without Eupheme, there's only Lady Tiamore ... Oh the beautiful Lady Tiamore, her Kingdom the last. And you know what they say ... the last one to fall falls the hardest."

"You lie," Norbert roared.

†

Outnumbered ten to one, it had been a deadly war of attrition. His people had been severely bloodied—tens of thousands dead or at death's door and just as many injured. The battle had been fierce. Yet they had withstood the onslaught through sheer determination and force of will. Unwaveringly, he had remained at the helm, inspiring his soldiers with his courage and his strength. And although stretched too thin, they held their lines. The enemy had not been able to breach their defenses.

As the enemy had flung missiles at them so their anti-missiles had struck them from the sky; as their legions of warriors, magicians, beasts, and mechanical terrors had marched across the plains and streaked across the sky and sea, they had fought on.

Sir Francis stood amidst his Pyrrhic victory.

Two events had tipped the balance in their favor—one arriving early, the other late. The early had been a warning that had come from the Harbinger: a warning given to Lady Tiamore of the amassing armies, which had enabled them to prepare; the enemy thus, had lost the element of surprise.

When defeat and victory were precariously balanced, when hope was almost gone, the other, totally unprecedented, thing happened: an army comprised of both Angels and Demons arrived.

Struck at their most vulnerable points, the hordes' lines snapped and they fled.

Thereafter peace agreements were quickly sought. Frantic diplomats and armies of lawyers and spokesmen stood ready. Agreements and contracts were signed and blood oaths sworn.

Sir Francis entered his Lady's tent to give her the news. "My Lady, it is over. With the help of Heaven and Hell, we have prevailed."

Lady Tiamore was busy gathering her things, preparing for a journey.

"My Lady," he asked, knowing already what she planned.

"Francis," she began, "I must find my daughter."

"Know that your present course is ill advised. You must reign over your Kingdom." The Knight spoke to her plainly and honestly. His words pierced her, making sudden tears spring from her eyes.

He continued, "Your place, my Lady, is with your people. We could easily have lost all of what we hold dear and true. Your lands have been damaged; your people have suffered great losses. For you, they have fought and it is from you that they now seek guidance and the wisdom to rebuild."

"My daughter," she implored. "I have faced many difficult situations, but to have to choose between my daughter and duty ..." she left her words hanging.

"Duty," Sir Francis answered simply.

Her voice rose almost to anger as she spoke to her Knight. "Do you think it matters what we have done here today? All we have done is to postpone the inevitable."

"We don't know that," replied the Knight.

"They will return. They will break their peace treaties. They only have to win once and we shall lose all. And my daughter is a weapon that they can use against us. Against me."

"My Lady," he answered, approaching her and pleading gently with her, "today ... today we have prevailed. It is enough."

She remained silent.

"I know the burden is difficult, but without your sisters ... you alone must represent the Three Kingdoms:, Eupheme's Sky Kingdom, Ezrulie's Mountain Kingdom, and your own." He paused, "I know your heart grieves. Allow me to go in your stead. I shall find Valerie and bring her home."

On his best charger, the Knight set out on his quest. Into near and far away places he searched. He went into dark and freezing lands, into hot desolate wastelands, and into places where fearful dragons protected their treasurers of gold and precious gems. Boldly the Knight searched, making discrete inquiries about a little girl and a dark creature.

He spoke with scorpions and beasts; he spoke with men, soothsayers, and those who delved into the darkest of arts. He searched the seas, and the highest mountains, and he spoke to wise old men who taught him how to compel even the solar winds to speak, and yet they too had not seen or heard of the little girl ... or the Harbinger.

And even after being released by the greatest Shaman who ever lived, Sir Francis searched into deep and mysterious places where men had never ventured, the dark lands of the Harbingers. And yet no one had news. He learned two things: that Belothemus had never returned to his realm and that there was no trace of Valerie.

The Harbinger, as promised, had hidden her well.

✝

Norbert was thrown off and his sword skidded from his reach. Out of breath, he paused while he faced his antagonist. It was close, but it was becoming obvious which of them was the better of the two.

"Brother, you and I are enemies, but our interests intersect. We are much closer than you know. Don't you see? We simply desire a new beginning."

"It's not the beginning that concerns me; it's the end part that I don't like," spat Norbert.

"Don't you want an end to this senseless bloodshed, which has ravaged and wrecked our kind, and kept them apart for thousands of years?"

"Bloodshed. We are responsible for our own bloodshed," muttered Norbert.

"We can remake things. Make things better."

"What? In your image, you ugly son of a bitch," scoffed Norbert.

"The possibilities! Valerie and Khia are destined to help us remake the worlds. We can close worlds that should never have been called into existence. Initium Exordium. A new beginning."

"So you'll destroy everything that has been. Good things still come from unlikely places. You are the fool, Burdock. The master you serve will destroy everything, because he cares for nothing."

"We must end it, Norbert!" screamed Burdock, circling his opponent and viciously striking out at him.

"I agree with you there," shouted Norbert, but Burdock was too quick. Thrown backwards, Norbert's back hit the wall with such impact, brick and stone collapsed upon him.

Burdock closed in and pressed his forearm roughly against Norbert's throat. While Norbert struggled for breath, Burdock stared into his eyes, "What has creation become? Look how far we have fallen! At least McBride had the wherewithal and fell with us when we were first divided."

Norbert gasped for air.

"You defend nothing!" Burdock screamed. "A system! A realm that has long ago lost its glory! Do you yield?"

Even without his sword, and at a marked disadvantage, Norbert refused.

Relaxing his resolve, Burdock expected Norbert to accept defeat. Burdock, you see, couldn't fathom why Norbert would not join their cause.

Pain racking his body, Norbert twisted to pick up a rusted piece of corroded steel that lay near him, striking out at Burdock, and missing his head by inches ... but it was enough to create some space between them.

"I was hoping you'd see it our way," Burdock snarled.

Avoiding the vicious, malicious thrusts and strikes of Burdock's blade, sweat poured from him. Driven relentlessly back, Norbert fell down a fifteen-foot drop and lay sprawled, face first in water and mud. He was in a section of the tunnel that had been bricked by workmen no less than a century before.

Burdock stood on the threshold, looking down on the one who had fallen. "Time is up. We need Khia. She is the key to freeing us. Norbert," Burdock grew quiet, "I didn't make the rules. These are the rules that have been foisted on us, and we are forced to live with. It's time we change the rules."

"You will not use Khia. I won't allow it."

Burdock laughed, "Oh, there you are wrong."

"Did anyone ever tell you, you talk too much," muttered Norbert. He saw a silver swirl that caught his attention. Miraculously, his sword had returned to him, once again, when he needed it most. Like liquid mercury, it moved towards him unseen through the cracks of the bricks and debris, glinting for his eyes only. Norbert saw the hilt of his blade take shape. It shone conspiratorially in the dirty water.

"Die then my old friend," said Burdock, like a high priest reading an edict from on high. "I shall see you on Judgment Day."

†

Very few lights lit the passage. Devon stumbled in the dark to keep up. McBride hoisted him up on his shoulder and urged Khia on.

"What about Norbert?" panted Khia. "Shouldn't we have stayed and helped him.

"Don't worry about him. He'll manage."

They came to a T junction. McBride hesitated.

"Which way do we go?" asked Khia, but McBride wasn't sure.

Khia closed her eyes and concentrated. To get a sense of their direction, she visualized their progress: getting off the train and the paths they had taken to get to this spot. But then, before them, appeared Timothea's Silver Wolf.

"This way!" shouted Khia, following the creature.

Minutes later, they saw a light above them. The large wolf stared at Khia and then vanished into the darkness. They climbed a steel ladder and McBride lifted the grate; they climbed onto the streets of New York City.

"You've got some very interesting friends, Khia," stated McBride matter-of-factly, as he lifted Devon out of the hole. "Come on."

†

When Burdock jumped, Norbert made his move.

With an incredibly fast roll, Norbert retrieved his sword from the stagnant water, and in an even faster sweeping underhand motion that cast a pall of water all around him, his blade flew in a graceful arc ... striking Burdock when he was at his most vulnerable.

Burdock knew he had miscalculated the moment he jumped off the fifteen-foot ledge. He knew the moment Norbert made his move. The sword struck him dead center. It pierced his leather jacket, pierced his skin and flesh, went between his ribs and right through his torso, and deep into twelve inches of old brick, mortar, and concrete—pinning him to the wall.

Burdock screamed, not only because of the intense pain but also because he had failed; his own sword fell from his hand, clattering to the ground.

"Damn you for all of eternity," Burdock cried out. He reached forward to try to wrest the blade from the wound, but the blade would have none of it. He was powerless. He reached up, with arms outstretched, to grab the ledge and so ease the pressure of his crucifixion.

"Initium Exordium," he rasped, spitting blood from his mouth. "We shall prevail; we will force the end of time and create a new Genesis."

"Do you hear yourself? Why don't you just shut up and contemplate your beliefs." Norbert left Burdock impaled by his sword, knowing that one of two things could happen: (1) If Burdock was freed, his sword would find its way back to him; (2) If he needed his sword, it would set Burdock free and find its way back to him. He hoped he wouldn't be needing his sword anytime soon.

A few minutes later, glad to be above ground, he caught up to McBride.

"You look a right mess," he was welcomed by McBride.

"Funny," growled Norbert.

"What happened to my friend back there?" asked McBride, in all seriousness.

"Oh, he had to hang around," responded Norbert.

CHAPTER 29

Grand Central Station

A few blocks from their destination, McBride asked the cabbie to pull over, and handed him a wad of greenbacks—not even looking at the denominations.

"No haggling, McBride? What's wrong with you?" teased Norbert.

"Time and place, Norbert," retorted McBride. He looked at Khia and Devon and said, "*Now* he develops a sense of humor!"

"I've always had a sense of humor," Norbert answered in a gruff voice.

"If you say so," laughed McBride, but quickly changed his tone as he looked around. "This isn't right."

The street was deserted. New York City, near Grand Central Station and the street, was deserted. Something was definitely wrong.

"Keep walking," demanded Norbert, as he and his partner placed their hands in the rucksacks they carried.

Across the street they could see the Station—the large opulent building with its towering columns that stood two by two, great windows, and a giant clock crowned by a marble angel. It was almost nine.

"Khia," Norbert said brusquely, "no matter what happens, you and Devon go through those doors. Understand?"

Khia nodded and squeezed her brother's hand.

"We're taking a train to Grandma's house?" asked Devon excitedly.

"Uh, not exactly kid," responded McBride.

They walked underneath the large metal bridge that led to the main doors of Grand Central Station. As their feet touched the asphalt … pandemonium broke loose.

Fortunately, Norbert and McBride were expecting it. Just as Goula and Dodger had forewarned, Blackwood mercenaries were waiting for them.

No longer deserted, the street started to come alive. From all directions, high beams blazed, as idling black cars with tinted windows moved in around them; SUVs and military vehicles took backup positions, forming a secondary ring. Anonymous figures dressed in fatigues emerged from the shadows with guns drawn. They heard multiple clicks—the sound of guns ready to fire.

As the clock struck nine, Norbert and McBride drew their weapons and blasted tires, headlights, and windscreens.

Simultaneous explosions near Blackwood's men caused the ground underneath to give way. A huge sink hole materialized and a plume of steam erupted.

"Thank you, Goula," McBride shouted to the sky, as he turned in a quick circle, shooting at anything that moved.

"They're good," praised Norbert.

"It's their numbers, not their skill," replied McBride. "It's overkill."

"I was talking about Dodger and Goula. Well placed and well-timed explosives."

"That last one could have been a smidgen to the left."

Amidst the chaos and confusion, Khia and Devon—protected between Norbert and McBride—hurried towards the entrance.

"Catherine," Khia stopped in surprise.

"What the hell is she doing here?" asked Norbert to McBride, as if he had something to do with this. He was none too pleased to see her.

Not many people can pull off wearing white leather, but Catherine the Great looked amazing. She was just outside the building's entrance, chatting with a security guard.

"Don't stop. Through the door!" shouted Norbert.

In-between two glass doors, Khia hesitated. Inside the terminal, on the other side of the glass, they could see a phalanx of mercenaries positioning themselves in two tight lines, weapons rising in their direction. Surely they'd be killed if they went into the terminal. She glanced backwards. There was no retreat either.

She tensed.

"Through the doors!" repeated Norbert, spraying a round of bullets that pierced the glass, breaking the mercenaries' regimental line.

Khia stumbled through the door, along with Devon, Catherine, Norbert, McBride, and a hapless security guard.

Expecting to be met with violence, Khia found herself in a large hallway, walking on a polished, teal-veined marble floor. From far away, she heard the muffled sound of a clock striking nine; a door behind her closed. Then everything became eerily quiet, except for their heavy breathing.

Where were they?

It was a darkened corridor that seemed to go on forever ... like when you look at two mirrors facing each other and see infinite reflections. There were doors of every shape and color, and in front of each and every door, a soldier standing perfectly still.

"We made it," laughed McBride. "Welcome to the Corridor of Doors, or if you want, the Hall of Eternity."

"You," Norbert directed his attention to the surprised security guard, "what are you doing here?"

The security guard, Kumar Singh (but everyone just called him Frank), looked around in confusion. He didn't know what to do. This situation wasn't covered in the manual's guide they provided to all employees.

"I ... I was ..." he stumbled over his words, "on my break. I was having a quick smoke," he said defensively, although he had actually been making conversation with Catherine.

"Don't you know that smoking is bad for your health?" asked Norbert. The security guard nodded but didn't move, blinking a few too many times.

"Well get out!" yelled Norbert.

"If you could point me in the right direction ..." he spoke meekly, "sir." Norbert shook his head, and walked up to a nondescript door.

The security guard hesitated. A loud rumbling noise in the long corridor prompted him to move. He put his hand through the door. It looked odd in the variegated light. He pulled it back again and said, "My friends will not believe this."

Through the door, they could see police cordoning off the area. Burnt vehicles littered the road and everything was dark and quiet. It was the aftermath of the explosions. Blackwood's men had disappeared without trace.

The security guard looked questionably at Norbert.

"Time moves differently here; read up on your relativity. Now get out," ordered Norbert gruffly, "or do you want to stay a security guard your entire life?"

Norbert eyes narrowed with impatience and pushed the man through.

"Tourists," Norbert commented.

"What are you doing here, Catherine?" asked McBride, concern in his voice.

"Your stories were true," Catherine said softly. "I had no idea. The news reports," her words spilled out hurriedly. "You told me the best place to find you would be at Grand Central Station. I've been here a week. I had almost given up, but when I saw an increasing number of agents roaming the terminal. I waited."

Norbert interrupted them, "Enough of the small talk. Reintroductions and explanations can wait. We have a job to finish."

Discarding his spent automatic, Norbert pulled out a couple of weapons that had been hidden under his coat.

McBride rummaged through the rucksack and tossed several weapons to Catherine.

Norbert looked questioningly at McBride. "Does she know how to use those?"

"Of course, we've had a few adventures together," McBride winked.

Their footsteps echoed down the long corridor. A few hundred feet ahead, one door began to glow.

"That's the door to your grandmother's world," McBride pointed out to Devon. It was a silver and gold door that was ornate and finely crafted.

Khia felt her heart jump in anticipation. Her grandmother! She really had a grandmother! She smiled, relishing the thought that there was indeed a person who cared for them enough to have sent Norbert and McBride to travel such great distances, to a different world, to find them.

Suddenly the lights in the corridor flickered on and off. In the growing expanding darkness, a malicious laugh reverberated along the hall.

"Ahhhh. I thought things were a little too easy," commented Norbert.

"Too easy?" exclaimed Catherine. "You've got to be kidding."

"See? Catherine thinks I have a sense of humor," Norbert said, looking at McBride.

"Not one step farther," commanded the female voice.

"Don't stop," countered Norbert, "Keep walking."

There was an upper level of doors. Six doors opened on the right side and seven doors on the left. Bright white light from thirteen different worlds spilled into the corridor like powerful stage lights.

A horrific creature, with bluish gray hues, fifteen feet tall, made of rock, and holding a great rock hammer, jumped down and landed hard in the Corridor, stepping into the light.

"A Rock Fury," said Norbert, as if that would explain it.

"And what is a Rock Fury?" asked Catherine.

"Stone creatures. Not very smart, they have rocks for brains, but if you get a few of these together they can be very formidable," explained McBride.

As if in answer, twelve more appeared. "Never seen so many together before," muttered Norbert.

"It seems that the end of our little game is upon us," came the haughty voice of Ezrulie.

Khia looked up and saw Ezrulie. She was standing on a balcony, surrounded by heavily armed bodyguards.

It was the woman in her dream—the woman who had tried to lure her from the bridge. It was the woman who had killed her father.

Norbert, sensing Khia's anger, gripped her arm. "Remember what I taught you."

Khia nodded. She had to control her emotions. If she acted impulsively, she knew she could get herself killed ... or her brother, or her friends.

Ezrulie issued a command to one of her bodyguard's. After a brief struggle, a woman appeared.

"Khia, Devon," pleaded Valerie, who looked tired and ragged, "come to me."

"Mother," whispered Khia, taking a step forwards.

Devon clung to Khia's hand. He didn't remember his mother.

"Okay, you can have them," spoke Norbert.

"What?" Khia said incredulously.

"It's not worth it. Risking our lives," said McBride, as Norbert shifted his position. "You can have them Ezrulie. They're too much trouble. Way too much whining. You should try getting these two to sleep at night." Suddenly, Norbert moved in a quick flash and shot a Rock Fury in the knee. With a loud bellow, the Rock Fury tumbled to the ground, its hammer skittering towards them.

"Just kidding," Norbert shouted to Ezrulie. Then to McBride, he said, "I'll handle this. Get the kids through that Portal. Now!" he ordered.

Mayhem descended upon them. Moving with the kids towards the glowing Portal, another Rock Fury blocked their passage. A moment later, it ceased to be a rock fury and became nothing more than shattered rock and debris. Catherine pressed her back against McBride's so they were better able to cover and protect each other and Khia and Devon.

"Don't hit Valerie," instructed McBride, and they showered the balcony with bullets. They succeeded in keeping Ezrulie and her crew down as they moved closer to the Portal.

McBride and Catherine turned and faced each other—weapons over each other's shoulders, lips separated by only inches. "I always knew you liked the adventurous ones," he said to her, while hitting a Rock Fury with multiple bullets.

"It's not because of the adventure," she replied, while shielding Khia and Devon.

"Why would you choose to be with me?" he asked, as men emerged from the shadows.

Catherine kissed McBride hard on his lips. "Because I love you," she answered. Why would you choose to be with me? she wanted to ask but the words remained unspoken.

In the meantime, Norbert sprinted forward and grabbed the hammer of the fallen rock creature. Turning in three great circles, like an Olympian thrower, he released the heavy hammer. It flew through the air and struck another Rock Fury, which shattered into a million pieces; rock debris tumbled everywhere.

Khia, holding onto her brother's hand, sprinted across the hall. A chunk of rock hit Khia on the arm as they ran over two very large crumbling heaps of debris. She winced. It would leave a bruise.

The Portal was only about a hundred feet ahead of them.

They kept running.

Fifty feet.

Twenty five …

As they got closer, it glowed brighter.

A man in fatigues, carrying an automatic weapon, jumped in front of Khia and Devon, blocking their path. Khia, without hesitation, reached into her boot and withdrew the knife Nora had given her. She threw the knife, hitting the man in the thigh. He fell, hitting his head hard on the marble floor; he was out cold.

Ten feet.

They were running up the stairs and the portal was opening. Khia saw a man dressed in armor of silver and gold. She pushed Devon through the Portal.

And then, Khia hesitated; she looked back. Red laser beams moved around like angry wasps crisscrossing the floor. She saw Norbert struggling to get up to the terrace, and McBride and Catherine, fighting back to back. The woman in white leather had felled another rock creature, which crumbled at her feet. And then Khia saw one red beam, steadier than the others, moving towards its intended target.

"Khia," she heard her brother's call. The Portal was closing.

"Khia," she heard him call again.

The Portal dimmed and clicked shut.

Khia retrieved her knife and boldly charged forward.

One of the red lasers found its mark. Khia screamed in warning, but she was too late. Khia heard a dull thump. A puff of smoke and blood exploded from Catherine. A surprised look of shock appeared on Catherine's face as she started to fall to the ground.

"Catherine!" Khia yelled.

McBride retaliated and shot the marksman with one bullet between the eyes.

Norbert, occupied with the Rock Furies, made his way closer to the balcony. The terrace supports, concrete and plaster showered about him. He pulled two bodyguards off the balcony. They fell over the edge into the corridor and were quickly stomped on and killed by the Rock Furies.

No longer liking the odds, that had been so decidedly in her favor, Ezrulie grabbed Valerie and fled, followed by some of her bodyguards. Just as Norbert climbed onto the crumbling balcony, the Portal they had escaped from, closed.

Norbert said nothing, but a moment later he flung himself off the balcony. The fight was definitely not yet over.

McBride carried Catherine as gently as he could, dodging lumbering Rock Furies.

"Khia!" Norbert cried out urgently. "Help McBride! I can deal with these things. Go. Get out!"

But he was seriously outnumbered. Two Rock Furies attacked and she watched as Norbert dove between them.

"Go!" he yelled.

Sprinting forward, she wrenched the portal door open. Carrying Catherine, McBride went through, narrowly escaping a Rock Fury.

They were outside Grand Central Station.

McBride cradled the bloodied Catherine in his arms.

"We've got to wait for Norbert," Khia said, tears forming in her eyes.

"We got to go. He'll find his way."

But Khia wasn't so sure. Norbert had put himself in jeopardy to save their lives. To save her life.

The next thing that happened—Norbert's powerful physique, flying backwards through the air, hit a parked car. A moment later, a massive Rock Fury with its stone hammer held high crashed through, but before it even had a chance, it disintegrated into a giant heap of rock and dust.

Few people have the ability to see such creatures. Because they don't exist on Earth, most people would simply see great slabs of stone crumbling to the ground.

As they staggered away from the station into the cool surreal night, Khia looked up at the clock with the marble angel guarding the station. It was nearing midnight, yet it had seemed like they had been in the corridor for no more than twenty minutes. Khia felt somewhat numb from her experience.

A taxi screeched to a halt.

"Get inside," shouted the driver, a black man with amber dreadlocks.

They jumped in.

"The hospital, I'll get you to the hospital," he spoke quickly. "I never knew those Rock Furies could enter our world. Man you must have really pissed someone off." He stopped talking when he saw Norbert's gun pointed at him.

"To the Cathedral. Now!" ordered Norbert.

"You need a doctor, not a priest. She's gonna die."

Norbert shoved the gun into his cheek.

"I gotta a first aid kit," said the taxi driver.

"St. Patrick's now," said Norbert.

"Okay mon, I'm cool. It's her funeral," responded the man, stepping on the gas pedal as the lights of New York City flickered off and on, and then went out.

CHAPTER 30

Sanctuary

The taxi driver put his foot on the accelerator and sped away. Weaving in and out of lanes, he veered onto oncoming traffic, shot onto the sidewalk (sending pedestrians scrambling), screeched around the corner, and came to a skidding halt in front of St. Patrick's Cathedral.

"I'm sorry," shouted Norbert to McBride, from the other side of the taxi as they scrambled out. "I didn't know our path would lead here."

McBride didn't answer.

The blackout that had descended upon the city had affected hundreds of city blocks. The Cathedral seemed to be the only place with light.

Khia sprinted up the steps and opened the massive door. When she turned around, she was surprised that the taxi driver was carrying Catherine.

A few steps behind were Norbert and McBride, covering their backs lest something else arrive.

They were barely through the doors when a great crushing sound came from outside. Abruptly, Khia turned, accidentally knocking over a large fount that held Holy water. Water pooled at her feet.

"No! No mon, I only had seven more payments!" cried the taxi driver, when he saw his crushed taxi. But when he saw the creature from hell advance up the church steps, he said no more.

He carried Catherine towards the front of the church, passing the Stations of the Cross.

Khia noticed an immediate difference in her guardians as they set foot in the church; it was as if Norbert was infused with a celestial energy, but in contrast, McBride looked pale and weak. The bald man stumbled and Khia reached out to hold his hand. Catherine's blood dripped from her wound, staining the marble floor. In front of the altar, the taxi driver gently placed Catherine down on the red carpet and compressed her wound in an attempt to stop the flowing blood. Visibly weak, McBride sat down beside her and cradled her head in his arms.

The church was beautiful, Khia thought. Hundreds of candles burned, casting shadows onto the sacred walls.

†

The Sylph growled angrily. It had followed Devon's scent all over New York City on a wild chase. When it had neared Grand Central Station it had lost the boy's scent and didn't understand why … but it had found another scent. The blood was a close match. It was close … It would seek retribution.

The steel hackles on its neck, shoulders, and spine rose. Euphorically, flexing its lean muscles, it drew itself up to its most terrifying height, preparing for a kill that would surely please its mother.

Entering holy ground, the Sylph immediately felt the difference in every cell of its body. Even though it had been long encased in holy ground before its birth, its shell had protected it. Instead of the comfort of heat, it tingled coldly. In the vestibule, it screamed in excruciating pain; it had stepped in the holy water that Khia had accidentally spilled.

Concealed in the vestibule of St. Patrick's Cathedral, Vatican guards suddenly emerged. Surrounding the beast, they raised their powerful assault rifles.

"Bullets cannot harm me," laughed the Sylph.

The instant the Sylph was hit, it knew its mistake. In its mind, it saw how the bullet had been made: from the iron ore scraped deep in the earth, the fire used to form its casing, the hands that had packed it into a box, and delivered it to a man in a long brown robe. Sitting at an old wooden table, an old monk read from an ancient book filled with elaborate rituals and prayers. With sure hands, the elderly monk filled the empty shell with powder and then dipped the tip of the bullet into a bowl that held a liquid that changed the bullet's tip into tarnished silver. The Sylph followed the bullet's journey and witnessed how it was given to a Papal Guard, who placed it into its chamber; it felt the clench of the soldier's hand and felt the bullet fly and shatter on impact … and it felt bitterly cold as the poison coursed through its bloodstream, moving to its heart.

The Sylph stumbled and crashed into the pews. Vatican elite guards surrounded it.

"Bind it," ordered a commanding voice with a Sicilian accent.

Khia looked at the commanding figure clothed in a long red robe, and beside him, saw a priest.

"Father Tobias," said Khia, with astonishment.

"Khia!" Reassuringly, he moved towards her. "You are safe."

The figure in the flowing red robe issued his edict, "Andiamo. Subito. We leave for Rome. Immediately."

The taxi driver took a few steps in an attempt to take his leave, but was stopped by the Vatican guards. "Oh," he said with a nervous laugh, "you mean me too! I've never been to Rome." He clamped his mouth shut.

Khia stood at the altar and looked around her. The Sylph was either dead or dying. The guards had placed it in a silver cage—its beautiful red and gold skin fading to brown. Norbert seemed to glow. She could see a golden aura around him. McBride, on the other hand, struggled to breathe, yet as far as she knew, he hadn't been injured. He looked gray and ashen. And Catherine; Catherine looked deathly pale, and her white leather seeped in red. She had lost so much blood.

"Clean this up," said the commanding voice. "This never happened."

"Yes, Monsignor."

Epilogue

A private jet sat on the runway at John F. Kennedy International Airport. Given clearance, it ascended into the heavens.

Looking out the window, Khia saw her reflection in the Plexiglas. Tears welled in her eyes. All the while she'd been so afraid that her brother would be taken away from her, and in the end it was she who had pushed him away from her …

Below, in the cargo hold … an angry thing dreamed tortured dreams.

Here ends

BeTwEeN † BetwIXt.

Printed in Canada